WHEN LOVE AIN'T ENOUGH 2

R. COXTON

Copyright © 2019 by R. Coxton

All rights reserved.

No part of this book may be reproduced in any form or by any electronic or mechanical means, including information storage and retrieval systems, without written permission from the author, except for the use of brief quotations in a book review.

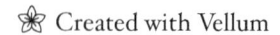

❦ Created with Vellum

Chapter One
I GOT YA

Thirty minutes later, Zeneka was pulling into her driveway when she saw a pair of headlights shining through her car. Not recognizing the car, she knew it wasn't Meech.

"Who the fuck is this?" she muttered to herself. Stepping out of his car, Rozay walked toward Zeneka's car. Alarmed, Zeneka reached in her purse for her mace. The tapping sound at her window made her jump. With the lighting in her yard, it made it hard for her to see that it was Rozay. She swung her car door open and stepped out, "Rozay, what the fuck you doing? You can't just pop up at my house. Why did you follow me?"

"Respect that I don't pop up on you at your shit," snapped Zeneka.

"I saw you all up in the next motherfucker's face," growled Rozay.

"Boy bye with that shit! I was vulnerable, we hooked up no more, no less," hissed Zeneka.

Zeneka saw some headlights in the distance then spat, "Hurry, you got to go."

Noticing the headlights as well, Rozay moved to head back to his car. Once he was there, with his hand on the door he growled, "This shit not over. Believe that."

Zeneka rolled her eyes. Rozay backed out of the driveway pissed off at her response.

"That bitch doesn't know who she fucking with," Rozay growled as he sped away.

***

After a restful night's sleep, Zeneka awoke to the sound of chirping birds and children playing in the neighborhood, both enjoying the Saturday morning bliss. Her mind went back to Rozay and his sudden possessiveness. Being that she was finally okay with her divorce, her pussy got wet at the mere thought of it. She was strategizing the changes she was going to implement in her life now that she was almost single. Zeneka knew that the football team would be practicing today at the school, so she had the perfect opportunity to get her class in order. Twenty minutes later, she headed downstairs to get in her car while Meech examined her outfit as she rounded the bottom of the stairs. He was staying at the house until his was ready.

"Damn, you are looking good! Where are you headed?" he

inquired, watching every move her body made, which appeared more beautiful now than ever before.

"I have to go to the school to pick up some things," she answered, making sure he got a full view of her outfit as she double-checked her lipstick in the mirror. She picked up her keys and headed out the door to her car. Meech stood at the door as Zeneka left.

"I know her ass on some sneaky shit," Meech muttered to himself, giving her enough time to leave.

Meech was already dressed. *What now,* he said to himself as he sat in his living room fuming.

"I got something for her ass watch me roll up on her ass." The more he thought about it, the more agitated he became.

Zeneka was excited about the possibility of seeing Jamari. She knew that Jamari had the keys to the school, so she would need to call him to get access to her classroom. The excitement had Zeneka bursting at the seams as she dialed his number. The phone rang for what seemed like an eternity and almost killed her spirits before he finally answered.

"Hello, this is Jamari. How can I help you?" he answered. His voice boomed in her ear. She was crushing on Jamari, but was skeptical because she and Meech weren't divorced, and Rozay's messy ass was lurking.

"Hello Jamari, this is Zeneka. I was wondering how long the team was going to be practicing today. I was hoping you could give me access to my classroom."

"We should be here another thirty minutes before we wrap it up," he smiled, excited at the fact he was going to see her again. "I can meet you at the main entrance in about ten minutes."

"That would be great! I should be there by then," Zeneka answered.

Unbeknownst to Zeneka, Meech was two steps ahead of her. As of late, he had been in the dark about Zeneka's comings and goings, so even though he was sleep deprived, he decided he was going to figure out what was really going on. He grabbed his keys and sat down in the CLK Benz. He activated the tracking app that was connected to both of their phones. After several minutes, the app located her at the school like she had informed him, but for her to be going on a Saturday, it wasn't adding up to him.

"Why the hell is she at her job on a Saturday much as she complains about it?" Meech questioned himself. He was hell bent on finding out the answer.

Zeneka stepped out of her car where Jamari, who was wearing an irresistible smile, greeted her. His reaction to her was the clue that her outfit had served its purpose. The skirt rode up her legs as she stood face to face with Jamari.

"My, my, aren't we looking delicious today," Jamari said as he took in Zeneka's ensemble and licked his lips.

"Nice to see you too, Jamari," Zeneka replied seductively as they both felt the sexual tension between them rise. "Well, are you going to let me in?" Zeneka asked as Jamari seemed stuck on her appearance.

"Can you let me into my class?" Jamari smiled.

"Well, on that note," Zeneka stated as she began walking

toward the door. Jamari followed close behind watching her ass, which she knew had his attention. She purposely wore the tight dress to outline her thong. Jamari figured he was part of the reason she was there, but he wasn't certain if that was the reason she was working on a Saturday morning. Her appearance caught him off guard. Jamari eyed her every move as her ass danced in her dress. "So, you trying to win teacher of the year?" Jamari joked.

"Well, since you must know, smart-ass, this was just one of my stops," she assured him. She was here to tease Jamari for the time being.

Zeneka wasn't about to play herself as some lonely, sex-deprived housewife in search of dick. By now, Jamari was inches from her ass, damn near slobbering at the mouth watching it bounce in a rhythmic motion in her dress. "You like that, huh," Zeneka chimed. Her plan was working. She knew she had his full attention as she looked back at his swelling bulge.

"I'm really enjoying the view from back here," Jamari stated as he grazed his swollen manhood against her ass as he walked around her and unlocked the door. Zeneka's facial expression told Jamari that he heard her loud and clear. The stiffness of his cock made her wet. Jamari clicked the lock, and they were in. Zeneka was surprised by his boldness but she had plans for him in due time.

"Would you like for me to check the building before I leave?" Jamari asked.

Zeneka knew it was time to play the damsel in distress, so

she politely declined. "I'm okay, but thank you," she said meekly."

Meech was stuck in standstill traffic caused by a bad accident ahead of him. He was getting more aggravated by the minute as the traffic crept along slower than a snail's pace. Meech was never one for Zeneka's daily routine, but now that her ideology changed, he was going to get to the bottom of what was really going on. It didn't matter if it took him all day long, in the heat, and standstill traffic. He was determined to find the answer.

Jamari asked Zeneka to remain in her classroom while he checked the building to be sure it was empty.

"Everything is clear far as I can see," Jamari stated as chauvinism oozed from his pores.

"Well, I'm grateful that you were concerned about my safety," Zeneka said as she walked into the class. Jamari was now fully engaged.

"Well, excuse me. I have to check on my team," Jamari said as he left.

Zeneka spat, "Well, enjoy your day." Zeneka loved the way his cock responded to her flirting. It made her pussy even wetter.

Meech had survived the forty-five-minute traffic delay and was pulling up to the school when Zeneka's car came into sight. He didn't want to be obvious, so he parked in the lower parking lot closer to the highway. He got out of the car and made his way to the hallway doors. He was surprised to see the doors unlocked as he pulled at them. He entered the building walking at a steady pace. Meech knew Zeneka's classroom was two halls over, taking notice of the quiet hallway as his footsteps echoed throughout the building.

Zeneka's concentration was broken by Meech's footsteps as his Air Jordan's squeaked on the freshly waxed floors. "What is that? I know Jamari checked the building," Zeneka questioned herself. As the steps got closer, she grabbed some scissors, but then she thought it could be Jamari coming back.

Meech entered Zeneka's classroom. He had followed her. She was packing up some stuff when he tapped on the door. Zeneka looked stunned at his entrance.

"What you are doing in here on a Saturday? You really love your job," Meech sarcastically snapped. Zeneka, aggravated by his appearance, slammed the boxes down. She couldn't believe his foul ass had

the nerve to pop-up on her with all the shit he had done throughout their marriage.

"Why are you here?" she asked. "I thought our business was concluded. Plus, you're my soon to be ex-husband."

"I'm still your husband till the ink dries," Meech laughed.

"I was making sure you weren't joking," she interjected. "You sure you want to fuck with me like this?"

"So, I see you fucking around with these clowns?" Meech fumed.

"Why you tripping? You been doing you, now I'm doing me," Zeneka said as she smirked at him.

Zeneka now pissed off chimed, "Now I'm a concern to you, boy bye."

Meech's ego was bruised by her truth. "Well, believe me, I will be out of your hair soon enough. Plus, I will be traveling more for the job," Meech huffed. "But I see you slinging that pussy like flapjacks."

"Honey, I learned from the best: your sorry ass. This pussy here is mine. You lost your rights," she snapped and giggled.

"Was that supposed to piss me off?" Meech joked. "So, sand niggers your flavor now?"

"We fucked one time. Stop being extra," Zeneka sighed.

"Oh, yeah I know you fucked Shanice's friend," Meech sneered. "You forgot my family runs this town? I know anything that pops off."

Zeneka's facial expression was priceless at his statement. *How the hell did he know about what I've been doing?* she asked herself. Meech smiled at Zeneka as she looked like a deer caught in headlights as her plan had blown up in her face.

"Why do you think I said what I said?" Meech smiled. "The struggle is real." Zeneka now deflated as Meech gloated at his minor accomplishment.

"Let me catch you with a motherfucker. I'm fucking both of you up on-site," Meech fumed before he left. "Until that ink dries, you're mine. Whether I'm around or not."

"Fuck you Meech, smart-mouthed motherfucker," Zeneka snapped.

"I love you too," Meech laughed at a pissed Zeneka.

Chapter Two
BOY BYE

*L*ucci peered out of the window as Shanice drove up in a gray Benz. He couldn't remember being this excited about a date. Walking to the car, he opened the door as she got out.

Walking to the door, he asked, "Was it hard to find?"

Lucci was wearing a blue and black Dolce &Gabbana, Massimo jean shorts, and a pair of gray, throwback Jordans. They took each other in, and their chemistry was prevalent. Shanice had apparently come directly from the office. She had on a navy-blue jacket with a green, multi-colored top that had navy accents. Her pants were navy and wide-legged with three-quarter inch cuffs. Her shoes were hella sexy. She must not have had court today because they were chocolate, high-heeled sandals that exposed a pair of Tangerine painted toenails. Her hair was pulled back into a bun at the base of her neck. Her looks took him. He reached out to give her a hug and at the same time took in her perfume. It was so intoxicating. He knew this woman was different, so he knew he had to treat her as such.

"I'm glad you came," he said. She was skeptical as he led her into the condo.

"Believe me, I was debating it," she answered. She sat on the plush sofa, he sat across from her rubbing his palms together as he stared at her beautiful oval face. "So why me? I mean, you have been whoring for a minute," she asked with skepticism.

He answered, "Because you have honest eyes."

"It wasn't my eyes that caught your attention," she joked.

"One-hundred. At the time, that's all I had to work with," he answered. Lucci then asked, "Can I get you something to drink?"

She asked, "What do you have?"

"For you, whatever you want?" he replied.

She figured she would challenge him. "I'll have a Mountain Dew."

"With ice?" he countered.

Shanice giggled, "So why am I so special?"

"Real talk? I want to see where this is going. I feel like it has potential. You're smart. You can hold an intelligent conversation. Most of all, you don't pull punches. I like that."

Shanice shook her head. Even though it was heartfelt, she was skeptical.

"Let me get that drink for you," he offered Shanice just sat back and took the bachelor pad in while Lucci went in search for her Mountain Dew.

Still in challenge mode, Shanice asked, "I don't like to waste time because for me it's precious, so are you really serious about a relationship?"

Lucci was quiet, then answered, "Listen, I'm grown. I don't have time to waste. I can blow smoke up my ass. I don't need to blow it up to someone else's." Shanice's skepticism was gone after he answered. Lucci then asked, "So what about me piqued your interest?"

Shanice, now relaxed, answered with a devilish grin, "Because I want to see if you're real." Lucci shook his head with understanding.

"See, no pulled punches. No whammies," Lucci said with a half-smile, half-laugh. Lucci could feel himself getting aroused by Shanice's presence, which was not uncommon when he was in the company of an attractive woman. Normally he would be able to suppress it, but he was having a hard time trying to focus with Shanice. He didn't want to make her uncomfortable on their first date.

Lucci could tell she was tired from work. "You can stretch out if you need to," he said.

Still not quite trusting this new relationship she answered, "Thank you, but I'm alright."

"I wouldn't bother you," Lucci said.

"Not worried about that. I'm a big girl," Shanice replied.

Lucci chuckled, "Listen, it's still early, and I want you in my space for a minute. I know you work long hours at the firm, so if you get too tired to drive home, I have a guest room. I wouldn't want you to have an accident. I'm invested here."

"That's abnormally sweet of you," Shanice said sarcastically. "It has been a rough week at the firm. You know we handle both criminal and family court cases. Since indictments should be coming down soon, some of the work has shifted. If I feel too tired, I will take you up on your offer," Shanice answered honestly.

"Cool, I'd feel better if you did. Don't want anything to happen to you," he responded. "Listen, if you want to get relaxed, I can find you some clothes to change into." Shanice gave him an *"I don't know you like that,"* look. Lucci smiled, "Best behavior. Seriously, I have a garden tub with the jets in it. It will help you relax."

"Let's see how the night plays out," she smiled. Shanice knew he could feel the heat between them along with curiosity. But from experience, she didn't want to tempt fate. "So, you telling me you haven't thought about getting serious with none of your other chicks?"

"Honestly, no because it was a casual situation," he answered with honesty.

"So why are guys like that?" Shanice inquired.

Lucci gave thought to his answer, "Because women tell you one thing in the beginning, and then later they want to change it. Guys are not made like that."

"That's some bullshit, you know that right?" she countered.

Lucci just laughed and said, "It is what it is."

"So, do you think we're going to fuck?" she asked.

Lucci was shocked by her bluntness. It sat him aback, but it was refreshing. "Honestly? I feel it will happen if I play my cards right."

"Listen, straight up – if we did, would you respect me in the morning, let alone want me to be your girl?"

"Not really," he answered.

Shanice respected his honesty. "Don't get me wrong, I love your swag, but I want to get to know you. I mean, we've been around each other for years, but I don't know the real you. For instance, what's your real name," she answered.

"Umm we would either need to be married or working on our first born before I ever reveal that type of information," Lucci said laughing. "But seriously, I'd like to see where this relationship goes because fucking the wheels off you right now would jeopardize what we could have."

Shanice was shocked by his honesty. "You right, I want more than that," she responded. They looked at each other in mutual understanding, and it was a surreal moment that neither was prepared for this early in the relationship.

Breaking the tension of the moment Shanice said, "Thanks for keeping it real with me."

"That's all I know is to keep it real," Lucci answered. Shanice was relieved at the conversation. "So, what do we do now?" Lucci asked.

Shanice was silent, then with a serious expression on her face, she said, "I guess we'll be two keeping-it-real-motherfuckers just looking at each other." She busted out laughing, rolling on his couch. She dealt with serious situations every day. She just wanted to be able to kick back with someone she could trust and build a relationship with and, of course, love. All that was way down the road. For now, the goal was to get through the first date.

Laughing, but having a better time than he'd had in a long time, Lucci was on board with their decision.

"So, does that offer for that bath still stand?" Shanice asked.

Lucci smiled and answered, "Yeah, whatever you want, Ma. Come on, I will run your water for you."

"Beggars can't be choosers, but are there Lush Bath products involved anywhere with this bath?"

Not missing a beat, Lucci said, "Nothing but the best for you, counselor."

As much as she hated to admit it, Lucci was right. He ran the water and asked Shanice to test the water to see if it was to her liking. He showed her how to set the jets to her taste and left her to her own devices. Every minute she sat in that tub; the worries of the day drifted from her shoulders. Using the citrus scented soap, she removed the dirt and grime of the day. He left some coconut oil on the counter, boy shorts, and a tank from Lane Bryant along with some Bath and Body Works lotions, but no drying towels.

Shanice was stepping out of the tub when thoughts of her and Lucci making love flooded her mind and tears filled her eyes Lucci tapping on the door interrupted her thoughts.

"Wassup? You okay in there?" Lucci asked.

"Where do you keep your towels?" Shanice asked.

"Look in the closet to your left," Lucci answered.

Shanice reached into the closet to pull out a plush towel. "I got me one," Shanice answered.

Lucci asked, "Is that all you need?"

"Yeah, thank you," Shanice answered. "I will be out in a minute."

Ten minutes later, Shanice walked into the living room wearing a black camisole top that fit perfectly and red and black boy shorts. He was even considerate enough to make sure she had a pair of flip-flops so that she wouldn't have to touch the floor with her bare feet. How he knew her size was a great question. Shanice knew that her ample ass would not be contained in the boy shorts, so she just charged it to the game. She hoped that Lucci had a strong constitution because she was going to push the envelope to see if he would stay true to his word.

Although he heard her approach because of the flip-flops, his back was to Shanice when she came into his family room. He was about to ask her what she'd like to watch, but got tongue-tied at the sight of her thinking, *"It's going to be a long, damn night."* Shanice missed his whole Elmer Fudd reenactment because she was rubbing her aching shoulder.

"What's wrong?" Lucci inquired. "You know I'm good with these hands. Want me to massage it for you?"

Shanice answered, "Yeah, if you know what you're doing."

Even after that wonderful bath, her shoulders and neck were still tense.

"Well, I will need you to lie down on my bed," he answered.

"Lead the way," Shanice said, suspicious but agreed. They made their way to the bedroom.

"Hold on, let me put some towels down." Lucci laid four towels across the bed.

"Okay, lay down." Shanice laid on top of the towels. "I have a special mix for muscle pain: Marjoram, Ginger, and Lemon Grass."

"Umm, you sure are quite the essential oil man. Depending on how this works for me, I may need some of that," she teased. Lucci lathered his hands with the mixture and slowly massaged her shoulder. It complemented the Lush soap she had used earlier.

"Is that too hard?" he asked.

"I'm surprised it feels really good," she answered. After five minutes, he was done, but she said, "Well you should give me a full body massage since you started."

"You sure you are okay with that?' he asked.

"Yeah, come on. I'm okay," she answered. Lucci lifted the tee midway up Shanice's back, revealing an ass that was round and tight, barely being contained in the boy shorts he laid out for her.

"Damn, your ass looks good in those boy shorts?" he teased.

"You never saw an ass before?" she joked.

"Shit, I have seen more ass than a pair of panties, but I'm going to need you to take those off if you want a full body message," he answered. Then he posed the question to intimately touch her body to remove her boy shorts, "May I?" Shanice nodded her head and began to pull the shorts off her hips and down her legs. He laid them to the side and looked at his canvas. Trying to suppress his unruly dick, Lucci poured the warmed oil lightly on her back and went to work doing what some considered he did best.

"Damn, babe I need this," Shanice muffled with her face buried in the pillow. He slowly moved the tee up her back as he massaged her body with ease.

"OOOOO, babe I love this. Don't stop."

It was getting more and more difficult for Lucci to maintain. He knew he couldn't let the massage arouse him, so after fifteen minutes, he acted like he was tired.

"I better stop before we get into some trouble," he answered.

Chapter Three
IT'S POPPING

Zeneka was sitting on the patio of Midtown Sundries enjoying a cocktail when Rozay walked up on her. "Hey, stranger! Long time no see," Rozay joked. They hadn't seen each other in a while since the fiasco in the driveway.

Zeneka sneered at his presence. "Not today, I can't do you today."

Rozay frowned at her then hissed, "I was just sitting at the bar. I happened to see you out here. I was coming to speak."

"Man take your ass back inside," Zeneka fumed, not trying to make a scene on the crowded patio. Rozay took a sip of his drink, smiled, and then teased, "Don't flatter yourself."

"I just want to chill and enjoy the vibe," she responded, now getting irritated. Rozay leaned across the table to grab a napkin. The sundress she was wearing was creeping up her thick, brown thighs, and he was all eyes.

"I see you are feeling yourself now," he smiled.

"No, I just don't want to deal with clown ass niggas like you," Zeneka smirked. Rozay pulled a chair from a table close by and sat down, only to aggravate Zeneka. Seeing he was in a petty mood, Zeneka grabbed her purse and drink as she stood up. "I see your bitch ass still on the same shit, so I'm going to slide," Zeneka huffed as she walked inside. Rozay found their banter entertaining as he watched her walk away.

***

Shanice sat up on the side of the bed and closed her eyes as she took in the feeling of the massage on her body.

"Are you okay?" Lucci asked. "I wasn't too rough, was I?"

Shanice just smiled and said, "No, just taking it all in. I liked that too much. It's just that it's been awhile."

"So, I didn't offend you, did I?" Lucci asked as he put the oil away.

"No, you didn't offend me," she answered.

"That's cool. I always want you to be comfortable around me," he answered. Do you need anything?" Lucci asked as he stood in the doorway as he led her into the house.

Thirty minutes later, Lucci and Shanice were in the living room watching Best Man when Shanice laid her head in his lap, stretching her body across the couch.

"Are you okay? Do you want a pillow or something?" he

asked.

"No, I'm good right here," she smiled. "So, are you trying to throw some hints?" she joked.

Lucci smiled and joked, "So, you got jokes."

"I just like the movie," Shanice smiled. "I like the fact that it shows black people in a positive light."

"That too," he answered. Shanice mentally stimulated Lucci, but at the same time, he was trying to deny his carnal urges.

Apparently, Lucci was having a really good time. His flag was being hoisted, and he was trying to play it off. You have to be blind not to see the swell of that mammoth dick. Knowing was half the battle, and she was so turned on knowing that she had this effect on him.

"You sure you don't need a pillow?" Lucci asked.

Shanice just smiled and answered, "No, I'm okay." Guys are always playing with the female mind. Shanice found this scenario as a prime opportunity to do the same to them for a change.

"Hold up for a second. I got to make a pit stop," he responded. Shanice sat up so he could excuse himself. As he did, she saw the imprint his dick was making in his jeans. She acted like she didn't notice, but the sight of it made her pussy wet.

"I will be right back," he responded as he excused himself.

"Okay, I will be right here waiting," she answered with a devilish grin on her face. *Let's see how the player plays this one off,* she thought to herself.

He made his way down the hallway at a steady pace. Once inside, he released his swollen manhood. "Damn," he muttered as he stroked it slowly. He was right at the point of ecstasy after stroking himself at a feverish pace. Lucci leaned against the sink as he exploded and felt the short waves of delight tighten his nut sack. "OOOO," was all he could get out of his mouth as he looked at his cum-covered hand. "Owe, damn I needed that," he murmured as he waited for his manhood to go down. After ten minutes, Shanice knocked on the bathroom door.

"Are you alright in there?" she asked. Shanice knew that her presence on Lucci's lap would create an arousal. She just wanted to see how he was going to handle it. Her panties were soaked from the excitement, but she was determined not to let on that she was just as aroused as he was.

"Yeah, just finishing up now," he answered, caught off-guard.

"I was just checking to make sure you were okay, that's all," she answered.

"I will be out in a minute," he stammered as he cleaned himself up. Lucci finished washing up and made his way back into the living room.

"Are you okay?" Shanice asked as Lucci sat on the recliner across from her. "So, you feel better now?"

"Yeah, I believe it was something I ate," he answered. Shanice just looked at him devilishly. "I'm kind of tired. I'm about to lay it down," he responded. Looking at her with a pained expression on his face he asked, "Raincheck?"

Chapter Four
PLAYTIME

*L*ucci sat back in the recliner and reached in the case and pulled out a blunt. He lit the blunt as he reminisced on the evening's events. He pulled out his phone and dialed Mesha's number.

"Hello, what you need?" Mesha snapped. Mesha was still very annoyed with Lucci, but he had something that most men didn't, so of course, she wasn't going to ignore his call even if she wanted to.

Lucci paused before answering. "What are you up too?" he asked.

"Nothing. Just sitting here getting wasted," she answered.

"You feel like coming through?" Lucci asked.

Mesha was silent, then answered, "I told you I was about wasted, "she answered.

"Catch a cab over here," he countered. "So, you'll come through?" Lucci asked.

"Yeah, you gonna pay for it?" Mesha was determined that something would work in her favor today; she figured that was the least he could do.

"Yeah, I got you," Lucci answered. In his mind, he knew Mesha wasn't who he wanted to be with at that moment, but she was always down for anything, and he couldn't let Shanice get in his head.

"Okay, let me call. See you in a little while," she answered.

Lucci ended the call and muttered, "I don't know who she thinks she's fucking with. Must think I'm some bitch ass dude."

Five minutes later, Mesha called back. "I called a cab, and it should be here in a few minutes," Mesha said.

"Okay, Shorty, I got another call. See you when you get here," Lucci responded.

"Okay, my cab out there. I'll see you when I get there," Mesha replied.

Clicking over, Lucci answered the phone.

"You told me to call you when I got home," Shanice replied. She really wanted to call on her way home, but after Lucci's final comment to her, she figured she would play it safe and see what kind of vibe she got from letting him know she was home.

"Oh okay," Lucci stammered. "Still not at my best. Was in the middle of something. Can I call you tomorrow?"

Lucci was acting weird and quite frankly, at this point,

Shanice could use a drink. Having already taken a bath at Lucci's, she headed to her bedroom to see if she could find something to wear and meet her girls.

***

Zeneka was still taking in the atmosphere of the Barksdale Winery and Lounge when Zania made her way back to the booth.

"Wassup, Jamari comes late," Zeneka joked.

"I'm glad you ladies let me hang out with you all," Jamari smiled. Zeneka was glad to see Jamari. It had been awhile.

Jamari just smiled and said, "So, you got jokes?" Zania knew Jamari from being on the club circuit.

"So, what's been happening?" Zeneka asked.

"Just working and learning this town," Jamari answered.

"Zeneka, why are you sitting there so quiet?" Zania joked.

Zeneka answered, "Just sitting here taking in the atmosphere."

Zeneka turned around and looked through the crowd and spotted Shanice.

"So, Zeneka, you're looking very tempting this evening," Jamari flirted as he scanned the room for a waitress. "So, is this winery new?" he asked as he stood to go to the bar.

"Wait. The waitress is coming now," Zeneka chimed as Jamari sat back down.

"Cool, I didn't feel like standing at that crowded bar anyway," Jamari said sarcastically.

Zeneka saw Shanice in the foreground. Zania was playing with her phone, and Jamari was watching the game from afar.

Barksdale's was filled to capacity. Zeneka was enjoying getting out of the house more. She was becoming quite the social butterfly.

"So, Zeneka, would you care to go to the wine room with me?" smiled a frustrated Jamari, longing for a drink.

"Sure, I would love to check it out," Zeneka smiled.

They both excused themselves, leaving Zania at the table by herself. Minutes later, they were downstairs in the wine room. Jamari was smiling from ear to ear as Zeneka sat across from him. "So, Ms. Zeneka, how have you been?" Jamari questioned. Zeneka was receptive to Jamari's flirting.

"Nothing much, just getting back into the swing of being single," Zeneka said. Between their banter, the waitress took their drink order. "What can I get for you all?" the weathered-blonde waitress said with a smile.

"I will have a Jack and Budweiser," Jamari spoke up.

"What will it be for you ma'am?" the waitress asked.

"I will have what he's having," Zeneka slyly smiled to the waitress.

"I will get that for you right away," the waitress said as she turned on her heel and left.

***

Back upstairs

Shanice had finally made it over to where Zania was sitting.

"Where did your sister go?" Shanice asked as she drank the citrus water.

Zania looked around the room then retorted, "I believe she went downstairs with Jamari."

Shanice smiled, and then oozed, "So, she must be really feeling him?"

Zania sneered at Shanice's words, "I believe she's down with whoever shows her ass some attention." Shanice frowned at Zania's words.

"Girl, you forever shading your sister," Shanice implied. "Those who live in glass houses should be careful of stones."

Offended, Zania asserted, "I ain't feeling this dead ass place, I'm about to be out." She grabbed her purse and rose up from the table.

"I hope I'm not the reason you're leaving," Shanice smirked and winked as she sipped on her citrus water.

"No, I'm used to unsolicited bullshit," she sighed as she left.

***

"So, you like it here so far?" Zeneka questioned.

"So far so good," he huffed.

They both were slightly tipsy and involuntarily smiling at each other.

"So, how is the transition going for you?" Jamari asked, concerned. "I saw your friend from the other night upstairs. Do y'all hang out all the time?"

Zeneka didn't want to come off like a party-girl after she had played so naïve when he had asked her about the nightlife before. "All of this is new to me," Zeneka uttered.

Jamari took in how the lighting enhanced her beauty.

"Man, you are truly beautiful," Jamari smiled.

Zeneka had decided that after dealing with Rozay, she was going a different route with Jamari. She was going to get to know him. She didn't need any more stalkers.

"Thank you," Zeneka blushed as she looked at her watch.

"Am I boring you?" Jamari joked.

"No, not at all. I just assumed that Shanice or my sister would've come down here by now," Zeneka assured him.

Relieved at her response, Jamari's jitters subsided.

"No, I love this setting it's more intimate down here," Zeneka assured him even more.

Hours passed as they laughed and talked undisturbed.

"Well, it's getting late," Zeneka cooed, now feeling the day catching up to her as she sipped on her coffee.

Jamari had enjoyed getting to know Zeneka outside of work. "Well, let me walk you out," Jamari said, disappointed.

As she grabbed her coat, she smiled and said, "We have to do this again when it's not a work night."

Minutes later, they were standing by Zeneka's car. Jamari moved in for a kiss while Zeneka fumbled in her purse. She lifted her head and leaned back as he tried to sneak a kiss.

"Whoa, no harm, but I'm not ready for that," Zeneka said as she backed away.

Embarrassed, Jamari pulled back and responded, "I'm sorry for being so forward."

"No problem," Zeneka giggled as she opened her car door, she leaned in and gave him a hug.

"Well, I will see you in the morning," Zeneka chimed as she sat in her car.

"Can you text me and let me know you made it home safely?" Jamari scoffed. Minutes later, all he could see was her taillights.

Chapter Five
I'M SO OVER IT

The next day at Shanice's office
Shanice just listened as Zeneka recounted all the misdeeds Meech had done to her.

"Listen, can't tell you I understand, but I'm here for you. You are a whole lot stronger than we gave you credit for," Shanice always knew how to be a good friend.

Zeneka pushed her drink to the side and ordered a hot tea and water. She had two vanilla rum and coke and wanted to make sure that she was straight driving home. Plus, that whole conversation with Jamari sobered her up. Zeneka knew that she would need to get her weight up when talking with him because he was well above her weight class. Listening to what Shanice said, Zeneka sighed and said, "I guess I'm at an impasse right now."

"I don't want to get into something that I'm just not

emotionally ready for. He's a good guy, but I would hurt him," Zeneka testified.

"I had to get into your sister's ass," Shanice interrupted.

Zeneka sighed, "What did she do now?"

Hesitant to go in depth, she just spat, "Zania being herself." Zeneka went back to talking about her evening.

"I thought y'all were going to come downstairs," Zeneka retorted.

"I saw y'all down there talking, but didn't want to disturb you," smiled Shanice.

"So, did you enjoy yourself?" inquired an excited Shanice.

Zeneka smirked then responded, "It's a work in progress."

"Well, enough about that. I have my paralegal drawing up divorce papers," Shanice assured her.

***

Zania and Rozay were on the dance floor gyrating and groping at each other. "Look at that shit there," Shanice said as she pointed to Rozay and Zania dancing.

Zeneka just rolled her eyes as she caught sight of them dancing. "If Shanice knew that Rozay was possibly digging me, why would she be putting herself out there like that? You know I love our girl, but that shit is shady."

Looking at them and shaking her head, Shanice thought to herself, *You don't know the half of her shadiness.* Having seen enough of the scene on the dance floor Shanice asked, "Hey, you about ready to get out of here?"

"Yeah, I'm tired. Plus, I ain't feeling the company anyway," Zeneka answered.

"I heard that," Shanice laughed as she looked at Rozay and Zania.

Zeneka gathered her purse and stood up to leave. They made their way to the door.

"You gone?" Zania yelled as they walked by.

"Yeah, I have an early morning," Shanice answered as they continued to the exit. Zeneka just smiled and waved as they walked.

"Well, I will call you tomorrow," Zeneka responded.

Ten minutes later, Shanice and Zeneka were standing by their cars. "So, what you going to do?" Shanice asked.

Knowing exactly what she was asking, Zeneka looked at Shanice and said, "I think I'm going to move forward with the divorce after our year is up. He'll be home tomorrow, so I'll listen to what he has to say. Based on the stuff that your private detective found, I don't think there's much to repair. The greater question is whether he will be honest in the financial settlement of our assets. He'd built quite a little nest egg with our money. I had no idea that we had two other rental houses. As long as he's fair, then I won't spank that ass in court," she added with a smile.

You wanna bunk with me while he gets his things out? I'm assuming he'd be moving and not you," Shanice asked.

"Naw. I'm not angry, but keep the option open just in case he does a 180 on me," Zeneka said laughing.

Shanice answered, "I understand, but the invitation is always open whenever."

Zeneka smiled and said, "You know I love you, right? I would be lost without you during this whole journey."

Shanice smiled coyly and said, "Reciprocated – Olay, call me when you get home."

Zeneka answered, "I will." She got in her car and pulled out the parking lot of the club. She had driven about three miles when she realized her gas light was on. "Oh shit, better not risk this not getting me home," she said as she pulled into a Quick Trip.

Zeneka pumped her gas and watched as the numbers on the tank quickly rose to almost $49 when a hand touching her free hand startled her. She screamed, "What the hell?" After recognizing the hand that had touched her, Zeneka said, "I was taught to slice first and ask questions later. Never walk upon a daughter of a Marine when she can't see you coming. You scared the shit out of me."

Jamari had deflected her swing, carrying a small blade. It was good to know she knew how to protect herself. Laughing and returning the blade he said, "I'm sorry, I was pumping on the opposite side when I noticed you pull up, do you need me to finish that for you?" Jamari asked. He moved in closer, and his cologne hit Zeneka's nose, creating a sensation in her body.

"No, I've got it," she said trying to regain her composure. She replaced the gas hose back in its chamber and moved around Jamari to get her keys out the ignition. He slid his hands slightly up her thigh as she passed him. "What are you doing here?" Zeneka asked, not sure what to say.

"I was already here pumping when you pulled up," Jamari responded. "When I saw you over there as I was about to go in and wash my hands, I figured I would see if you needed a hand first. I'm sorry if I startled you. That wasn't my intent. You handled yourself well though. So, your dad was a Marine?"

"Oh, it's not a problem, and yes he was a Jarhead," Zeneka said with pride. "He served in Vietnam. Infantry," she said as she closed the car door to head inside the store. "I need to use the restroom, and then I'm headed home. How about you?"

"Would you join me for a cup of coffee or a cappuccino? I heard of this place called Edith's in Kannapolis. From what I understand, they have really good beverages, and the food is on point," he said.

Zeneka smiled because she knew the place well. Hell, she spent most of her teenage and college years there during the summer.

"I know it's not a Starbucks or Panera, but I'd like to talk for a bit if that's okay?" Jamari said.

"Well I don't see any harm in coffee, after all the alcohol I drank tonight, it can't hurt." Zeneka replied. "Let me use the restroom really quick I will be back out. I actually live in Kannapolis, so it won't be out of my way."

Chapter Six

SECOND CHANCES

Edith's was a local restaurant in North Charlotte and it was by I-85 that also took you to Kannapolis. It took about twenty-five minutes to get there. Hopping out of their respective cars, they headed to the door of Edith's. The chime rang overhead, and a voice rang out behind the counter shouting, "Welcome to Edith's!"

Zeneka smiled and said, "Hey Uncle Matt!" Coming from around the counter, Uncle Matt approached Zeneka at full steam and grabbed her up in a bear hug, squeezing her tight.

Placing her in front of him so he could get a better look he said, "Hey, baby girl. Why are you out this late? Shouldn't you be at home?"

Zeneka dipped her head in embarrassment. No matter how old you get you will always be that "little girl" to those that helped raise you. Smiling she said, "No, sir. My friend heard such great things about Edith's and wanted to come for coffee."

Uncle Matt looked the newcomer up and down with a weathered eye and said, "Good evening, young man. Haven't you visited us before?"

Embarrassed by the revelation, Jamari responded, "Yes, sir. Your place reminds me of my mother's cooking, and to be honest, I've been homesick."

In an attempt to ease her Uncle's interrogation, she asked sweetly, "Uncle Matt? Can you get me a small, hazelnut coffee with some carnation milk and three sugars? Oh, and some whipped cream? We'll seat ourselves."

Zeneka handed Jamari a menu just in case he wanted to order something. Within a few minutes, Uncle Matt brought over her requested drink and sat it gently on the table saying, "Here you go. I thought a large was just as good as a small. Be careful. It's really hot."

Shaking her head, Uncle Matt always spoiled her. He gave a small cup to Jamari saying, "Here you go, young blood."

Nodding his head in thanks, Zeneka and Jamari stirred their coffee in silence. Jamari broke the silence by asking, "Uncle Matt?"

Zeneka looked sly when she said, "Umm, my family actually owns this diner. It's been in our family in different forms since World War II. My great grandpa was a cook in the Army, and when he got back stateside, he couldn't find work. So, he opened Edith's, named after my great grandmother, and has been feeding the masses ever since."

"That is so dope!" Jamari said with genuine excitement.

"Thank you," Zeneka replied, trying hard not to burn her tongue. "So, what're the chances of both of us being at the same club and the same gas station in one night?" she asked with a giggle.

"I know, right?" Jamari said. "I'm glad that it worked out that way, I haven't been able to get you off my mind since that day you dropped your papers all over the hallway."

"Seriously?" Zeneka asked, surprised. "Are you always this forward with a woman you barely know?"

"No," he replied. "Only when I see something I want."

Trying to break the tension, she asked if Jamari wanted to go out to the patio. Partly because she needed to get some cooler air due to the heat the conversation was generating, and partly because Uncle Matt was looking like he was about to snap, crackle, and pop because Jamari was leaning in too close for his comfort.

Outside, Jamari had moved a lot closer to Zeneka as they sat on the circular concrete seats that were damp from the evening dew. He placed his hand on her knee and slipped it under her dress. "Are you okay with the fact that I want you?" he asked.

Shocked at his boldness but aroused by his touch. Zeneka looked into his eyes and could tell that not only was he genuine in his motive, but adamant that he was going to get what he wanted. She allowed Jamari to continue to move his hand up her thigh as her pussy begin to tingle in anticipation of its journey.

"I hope you don't want me to stop," he began, "because I've been wanting to taste you as I watched you in the club tonight. May I?" Even though they were outside, there were security cameras. Zeneka was tempted as Jamari's fingers continued up her thigh and were almost at her apex when she came to herself.

"We can't she said breathlessly," nodding her head towards the camera.

Jamari leaned over and kissed Zeneka's cheek and said, "I'll need a kiss before we leave."

Waving at her Uncle who was now standing at the large window watching their actions, Zeneka responded, "I'm going to have to give you a rain check on that."

Looking at her as if she had just signed an irrevocable contract, Jamari said without flinching, "I'm going to hold you to that." Never changing the stance, he was holding, he took her hand and kissed it.

Chapter Seven
AFTER THE MORNING AFTER

It was six o 'clock in the morning when Lucci rolled over to check the time. He knew at that time of the morning; Shanice would be getting ready to go to work. He stared at Mesha as she lay beside him slightly snoring with her mouth partially opened. She was still fully dressed, lying lifeless. *What the fuck was I thinking,* he thought to himself. He knew he had to call Shanice to make things right. He slipped out of the room and made his way into the living room to call her.

He dialed her number. After three rings, she answered, "Hey, how are you this morning?" Lucci was silently thinking she would still be hung up on the night before.

"I'm good," Shanice said in a very pleasant voice.

"I had you on my mind, so I decided to call," he answered.

Shanice smiled to herself as she said, "Well, it's good to know that I'm on your mind this early in the morning."

"Also, I wanted to apologize for last night," Lucci said, attempting to sound contrite.

"Boy, please, this is a whole new day. That's the past," she joked. Shanice hoped that if she blew it off as water under the bridge that they could start back at a good place.

"So, what are you doing? Getting ready for work?" he inquired.

"Nope, I don't have to be at work until 3:00," she answered.

Lucci knew he had to make things right between them, so he said, "Have you ever had a picnic in the park?"

Shanice was truly flattered by the thought and answered, "Can't say that I have." *Maybe he really does like me* she thought.

"Want to meet later for one?" Lucci asked. Lucci knew this may be his last opportunity, and since she was so nice about forgetting his dumb behavior last night, he was trying hard to make this stick.

Shanice answered readily but didn't want to sound too eager, "Yeah, that's fine."

"So, can you bring the ice and drinks?" he asked.

"Yeah, I can do that. What time are you talking about?" she asked.

Lucci paused because he knew he couldn't half ass this event. "Want to say around 11:00."

"Yeah, that would be fine," she answered.

"Okay, we'll meet at Walker Park at 11:00," Lucci reiterated. "So, what are you going to wear?" he asked.

"I will probably wear some shorts," she answered.

Disappointed, Lucci said, "Oh okay."

Shanice paused, "Why, what's wrong with shorts?"

"Nothing, just figured you would wear like a dress or something," he answered.

"If I wear a dress I know you will be all up under it," she joked.

"You right, we would probably get in trouble if you did," he answered. "Okay, just surprise me."

"Boy, you better stop putting dirty thoughts in my head," she teased.

"Well, I guess we must be thinking the same thing," he joked.

"Well, I'm about to lay back down. I will see you at 11:00," she answered.

"Okay, I will see you then," he answered." I'm looking forward to it and to seeing you."

***

Zeneka woke up with a booming headache from all the Crown Royal and rum she had drunk. *Damn, I feel like shit. Won't be doing that for a while no matter how bored I am,* she said to herself. Zeneka looked at the clock. It read 9:15. *Dammit! I can't believe I slept that late,* she grumbled to herself. She jumped up and said to herself, *I have to call my job.* Zeneka scrambled for the phone and called her job.

"Yes, this is Mrs. Barksdale."

"I'm running late because I'm a little under the weather," she coughed.

"Don't worry," Agnes, the office manager, answered. "I knew when I didn't see you by 7:30 that something was wrong, so I went ahead and got you a replacement. So, get better, and we will see you tomorrow if you feel up to it."

"Thank you, I really appreciate that, Mrs. Agnes," she answered.

"Alright, feel better," Agnes said as she ended the call.

Zeneka went back to lie down for a few more minutes. As she lay on her back with her face towards the ceiling, she couldn't help herself as tears began to stroll down her face. *"What is wrong with me?"* she mumbled to herself, pulling a pillow over her head. "First Rozay, and now Jamari! I'm no better than Meech with all his whores," she yelled, even though no one else could hear her.

Zeneka hadn't developed feelings for Rozay, or at least she thought she hadn't, even though they only slept together once. She could be woman enough to admit that his dance-capade with Zeneka did have her feeling some kind of way. If she looked at her feelings really closely, she would say it was jealousy, but what rights did she have? After all, she didn't really have a right to be mad. She had pushed Rozay away, but he didn't have to respond by groping her sister on the dance floor all night. It was like he wanted to make Zeneka jealous because she couldn't make a decision about him.

Zeneka was another matter. What really made Zeneka salty was that Zeneka knew she was feeling Rozay, but she was groping him like she was checking for ripe fruit – and now Jamari? He, on the other hand, was a completely different story. He was confident, sexy, and he didn't give a rat's ass if she was married.

For years, Zeneka had dressed as conservative as possible. The only compliments she received were from Meech on rare occasions and from her girls or her parents. She was honest enough with herself to admit she was feeling him. The problem was that Zeneka just wasn't sure of his intent – if he was truly feeling her, or he just wanted to fuck her.

After last night, Zeneka couldn't get Jamari out of her mind, and the weird thing was she hadn't even kissed him. She was learning that intimacy was an addictive thing. It wasn't just about the sex. It was also about being in someone's space and sharing each other. Just the thought of that prospect with Jamari had her horny as hell. The way he licked his lips made her think of other things, but as much as she was attracted to him, she learned from Rozay that it had to have more substance. She didn't have any expectations. As far as Jamari, she was taking it one day at a time.

***

Lucci was in the kitchen preparing the meal for his picnic with Shanice. He had awakened Mesha and put her in a cab so he could focus on his outing with Shanice. He wanted to take his time with the meal so that it would be on point. As he was putting the final touches on the meal, he looked at the clock. It was 10:35. He grabbed up the bag that contained the food and headed out the door. Fifteen minutes later, he arrived at the park where Shanice was waiting. She got out of the car after he pulled up. *"Wow"*, he muttered to himself as she stepped out of her car.

Shanice smiled as she looked him up and down. He was wearing a striped, purple Polo shirt, denim shorts, black Reeboks, and matching, purple face, Seiko watch. She was wearing a multi-colored dressed that made her skin glow. Trying to play it cool, he directed her to a picnic table.

"So, you really put all this together?" Shanice inquired.

"Yeah, what? I got skills like that," he chuckled. Shanice was impressed as he pulled out the food from the tote bag. "I know how to be romantic when I want too," he joked.

"I'm impressed," Shanice smiled. Lucci smiled as he opened the containers and told her to help herself as he handed her a plate. The menu consisted of turkey meatball subs, salad, and watermelon.

Thirty-minutes later, they were finished eating when Lucci responded, "Let me clean this up, and we can take in the park." Lucci had picked the perfect place because the traffic was slow, except for an older lady jogging.

"Okay, that would be nice," she answered. Lucci cleaned their plates, packed up the leftovers, and put them in his truck. They made their way down a trail that led to a pond and a bench. They sat down. "So, what brought on the picnic idea?" Shanice asked.

Lucci was silent before he answered, "Well, I always wanted to do it, just never had the right person to do it for." Impressed, Shanice just smiled. "So, you want to finish taking in the park?" Lucci asked as they made their way through a winding path that led to a bridge, which had a view of a highway. "So, what you thinking?" Lucci asked as he wrapped his arms around her waist.

"Nothing, I guess this scares me," she answered.

"Then, you're in good company because I'm scared too," he agreed. "I mean this whole love and relationship thing is new to me," he said. Not ready to face her directly as he talked through his feelings, Lucci stood behind her, but he could feel his dick getting hard, so he eased off of her.

"What's wrong?" Shanice smiled coyly.

"Nothing," Lucci answered as his dick pressed against his jean shorts. Shanice noticed the bulge in his shorts but played like she didn't notice. "So, what are we doing?" Shanice asked.

"I thought we were trying to get to know each other," he answered trying to distract her from noticing his arousal. Shanice just turned around as his arousal subsided. He took in her ass as she did. He pressed up against her. She felt the now semi-hardness of his dick through her dress as he toyed with the material. Not realizing he was so turned on by her in general, eventually led to him playing with her. He really wanted to see what kind of panties she had on. From what he could tell, they were black silk with a matching bra. He slid his finger inside her panties to see if she was just as aroused as he. Her nectar felt like baby oil on his fingers as he probed inside of her panties.

"Alright, babe don't start something you can't finish," she responded. They were in a somewhat secluded place in the park. Traffic was next to zero so Lucci made his move. There was a still, small voice that told him to hold back, but he ignored it and went with his heart. He was man enough to admit that he wanted her – bad; and if she was willing, then he would have her. He pulled her panties down slowly, giving her enough time to decline his advances before it was too late. He slightly bent her over the railing, and he slid into her hot pussy and didn't move. He should have listened to his head.

There was no way in the world that he was going give this up – ever. She was so wet and tight. He was afraid if he moved, he would cum. The pussy was just that good. Worried that something was wrong, Shanice began to push back.

"Stop. Don't move," Lucci said in a strained voice. In all his years of being sexually active, never had he been on the edge of wanting to cum so badly. He was about to shame the family.

Shanice was thinking something was wrong, so she didn't question his statement. He had her in a place between pleasure and pain. All of his length was filling her up, almost past capacity. It felt so good, she wanted to scream. If he didn't move, she was going to lose her mind.

Lucci was teetering on edge and had to keep saying over and over, "Her pleasure, and her pleasure." Then she moaned, and he broke. He literally began to fuck her to within an inch of her life. He had never been this uncontrolled in his life, and he was grateful that she trusted him enough with her body to know that he would not hurt her. Shanice moaned softly with each stroke, which just amplified his pleasure.

Shanice was losing a little bit of her sanity with each stroke. Shanice whimpered uncontrollably. It was as if he beelined to her erogenous zone and took that bitch captive. She was right there on the edge when he reached up, grabbed her nipple, twisted then pulled. Her wail of ecstasy caused birds to fly up around them. Lucci was right behind her literally and figuratively with a moan, "Shit," as he came harder than he had in ages.

"Wow!" was all Shanice could get out once she got her composure together. She couldn't remember a time that her body had been loved that well. Lucci gently slid her dress down and used his closeness as a cover to arrange himself.

"I guess I was just wanting a sample," he joked.

Shanice just looked and said, "Hell, if that's your sample I can only imagine what the full course meal would be like!"

Lucci just smiled and answered, "Come on, let's get out of here before we really get into trouble." They started to make their way through another path that led back to the beginning of the trail.

Arriving at the opening in the trail, Lucci took her hand and said, "I never wanted you to think it was all about sex with me and you. I really care about you." Lucci's statement put Shanice at ease because she didn't want him to think that she was like the other women he had dealt with.

She said, "This time with you has been surreal. Thank you for the unique experience."

"I know – me too. I believe it's a turn on knowing you might get caught," he joked, trying to ease the tension.

Shanice just smiled. Lucci knew that he never wanted to give her the impression that she was like the others.

As they reached the top of the trail, Shanice asked, "So what makes me different?"

Lucci squeezed her hand and joked, "One-hundred, because I love your big ass tits." Shanice took the joke in stride and said, "One-hundred, why?" Lucci answered without hesitation, "Because you see the real me." He was on new ground, showing his vulnerability.

Shanice joked, "So, after today you still going to call, right?"

"My day wouldn't be complete if I didn't," he smiled. His comments were heartfelt as they made their way back to their cars. Lucci took Shanice and pulled her to him for a goodbye kiss.

"Okay, babe call me later," Shanice said as she got into her car.

"I will. Listen, I really enjoyed the day," Lucci said again.

Shanice smiled and said, "I did too," as she drove away.

Chapter Eight
COMING HOME

Meech pulled out his phone and dialed Lucci's number. He answered on the fourth ring. "Wassup, big bruh, when you coming home?" teased Lucci.

"Hell, I got a psycho on my hands," Meech joked.

"Quit playing," Lucci responded.

Lucci laughed as Meech told him about his escapades on his trip. "So, that chick Pleasure? Ain't she like your boss or something?" Lucci asked.

"Whatever, you met her at the company cook-out. Remember, big ass but even bigger mouth," Meech said.

"Ohh, yeah, she was a five with a dime ass, okay. So, you think she gonna get at you?" Lucci inquired.

"Naw, that pussy riding somebody else's dick right about now," he answered. "Those broads try to make you think you are the only one when really you don't give a fuck as long as you are getting your share of the pussy."

"I know right. Keep it simple," teased Lucci. "Then they get mad when you don't give a fuck. So, tell me was that ass good?"

"Who?" Meech asked.

"Pleasure."

Meech paused for a minute then said, "Hell no. The anticipation is better than the pussy. Don't get me wrong, pussy wet as a bucket of water, but she a runner," he laughed.

"So, all that ass and she can't take a dick?" Lucci asked.

"Plus, she quiet as a church mouse. Hell – so that killed it for me."

Lucci burst out into laughter and said, "With all that mouth. Funny shit there. So, when do you touchdown?" Lucci asked.

"I will be home today. You still fucking around with Mesha," Meech inquired.

Lucci was quiet, then said, "Naw, right now I'm kicking it with this shorty I met a while back."

Meech paused and said, "Bruh? What? She got you fucked up like that?"

Lucci laughed the comment off and said, "She cool people."

"Man quit tripping, ain't nothing better than some new pussy," Meech said.

Trying to change the subject Lucci asked, "So, do you have a ride home from the airport?"

"Yeah – gonna catch an Uber or a cab," Meech said.

"Well, listen I'm about to jet out. Hit me up when you get back," Lucci responded.

"Alright peace," responded Meech before the call ended.

The flight was only an hour and a half, but Meech couldn't help but think of the last conversation that he had with Pleasure. She ran him down on the way out of the hotel on the last day. He was about to jump in a cab to the airport. He always knew that he wasn't man enough for Pleasure, and now he understood why. In the whole scheme of things, he really didn't care. Her business was her business.

"Baby, I'm so sorry. It was a mistake," Pleasure pleaded.

"Why didn't you tell me?" Meech countered as Pleasure regained her composure and the embarrassment dissipated.

Looking around to see who was watching their conversation she said, "I was scared that I would lose you."

Meech responded, "I'm not mad. Real talk? I suspected that you liked women, I was just waiting for you to feel comfortable enough with me to tell me."

Pleasure avoided eye contact with Meech as she said, "I was embarrassed to admit it."

"I thought you told me you were strictly dickly," he responded.

"Meech, I was just curious. I'm not gay – just curious," Pleasure pleaded.

Meech just shook his head. "Right, you're bisexual, and that's okay."

Pleasure was shocked at this revelation. "How did you know? I mean, what gave me away?"

Meech responded, "Baby, I have dealt with all kinds of women in my lifetime. I knew, but I thought eventually when you were comfortable with me, you'd tell me."

Pleasure still overtaken by embarrassment said, "Meech, I'm not gay."

"Right, because you're not exclusive to women. You like men as well. Again, I don't sit in the seat of judgment of what folks do in the privacy of their own bedroom."

Pleasure stood silent. Meech, being a smart ass, asked, "So what's up with us? So, when are you going to admit it? I mean, I won't be mad."

"Meech, I do love what we shared, but I was curious," she answered. "Besides, it's not like you're not married."

"Pleasure, please tell me the truth," he responded.

Pleasure was silent after the question was asked, but then said reluctantly, "Yes, I'm bisexual."

"Now, how hard was that?" he asked. "Why were you embarrassed? So, you would rather sneak around and hope that nobody would find out?"

Pleasure knew she was wrong when she answered, "I just thought that you wouldn't accept that part of me."

"I told you I loved what we shared. Every time we were together you made me feel what we shared. I love your drive and have learned a lot from you, I'm just not in love with you," Meech said solemnly.

Pleasure answered after thinking about it for a moment, "I just figured you wouldn't understand. I mean, I'm a good person."

"Your sexuality does not determine how good or bad you are as a person, it's just a part of you. You coming out would not have diminished what we shared. Just wish you would've felt secure enough with us to tell me," Meech answered.

"I know I want to be with you," Pleasure pleaded.

Meech placed his suitcase in the cab and turned to Pleasure and said, "Either way we're cool, and if I were honest with myself, I could say that, including my time with you, was what tanked my marriage. I should have been stronger to resist your tempting body," Meech said laughing, eliciting a smile from Pleasure. He continued on saying, "I think that maybe you have some things to figure out. Tell you like this as a friend, anything you have to hide ain't worth doing."

Pleasure, brokenhearted and embarrassed, still answered, "I understand."

"When we get back, just holler. You know I'm always down for a free lunch," Meech said smiling as he got into the cab that would take him to the airport. Before closing the door, he said, "Oh yeah, please tell your stud to back off. She's been following me ever since I saw you two together."

***

Meech exited the cab. He double-checked his boarding pass as he prepared to make his way to the concourse. He thought about how he started relationships on a positive note, but eventually they all crashed and burned.

He had always told himself that he didn't want to be like his father, but he knew he was traveling the same path. He knew the best thing he could do for Zeneka was to give her whatever she wanted in the divorce. He felt like she deserved it. She had always been a good wife to him even though he never reciprocated by doing right by her. He knew that his philandering over the years had created the women he left before his business trip. *"Man, I really fucked up a good thing," he thought to himself.* Plus, he knew sooner or later she would find out about him and Zeneka.

Before the pity party could set in, he heard them announcing his flight as he made his way to the boarding ramp. Meech slept off and on as the plane left the tarmac. He knew he had a long flight ahead of him. After boarding the plane, there was a thirty-minute wait. He wasn't looking forward to going home, but he knew it was something that had to be handled. He knew it was the right thing to do.

***

Meech arrived at home and was nervous for the first time in a long time. He didn't bother calling her for pick up, just grabbed a cab. Besides, she would be in class anyway. It gave him more time to think about what he was going to say.

The conference in Savannah, Georgia was really good. It helped him make more contacts and he actually learned a lot about new shipping technology. Gone were the days of calling up a stockbroker and placing your trades. Meech was actually licensed to trade both stocks and mutual funds but found that there was better money in working for his family, and less headache.

Though he was ending a marriage, he was happy about the possibility of the new one that was budding with Neeka. He had been out of her presence less than twenty-four hours, and he couldn't get her out of his mind. She really was a sweetheart, and he wanted to take his time to make this relationship work, no matter how long it took.

Pleasure, on the other hand, was turning out to be a problem. He really didn't care what she did in her spare time, whether it was with a man or a woman. After all, the only person he really cared about in that respect was Zeneka – until Neeka came along. That nut actually tried to get Neeka fired. She was off the chain. To add insult to injury, after he saw her strapped up wearing Pleasure's ass out, her stud kept popping up when he and Neeka were out at random places. All of it was weird actually.

Meech considered himself forward thinking when it came to relationships. If you were exclusive, then, of course, you could be upset if one person stepped outside of the relationship – whether it was a man or a woman. Maybe it was all about control. Pleasure liked to control everything around her. She was even a drill sergeant in the bedroom. Reflecting on their time together, he recognized she held all the cards. The ironic thing was, she really didn't want a man, but rather wanted a woman all this time.

In the whole scheme of things, he had more important

things, like the dissolution of his marriage. After paying the Uber driver, Meech grabbed his things out of the trunk. Wheeling his luggage up the drive, Meech used his key and said under his breath, *"Time to face the music."*

Chapter Nine
LET'S GET READY TO RUMBLE

Shanice was stomping down the hallway after she had gotten her earrings as a matter of fact, she yanked said earrings out of Mesha's ears, who was wearing them as if she bought them. All Shanice was trying to do was to put some time in with Lucci. She should have stayed at home. Mesha had been posting subliminals on social media as well as sending Shanice reckless texts through messenger.

Lucci was sitting on the couch laughing at the play-by-play between two women fighting over earrings. He stood up and rushed past Shanice, blocking the end of the hallway.

"Get out of my way, Lucci!" she yelled.

"Lucci, let her go if she wants to go," Mesha chimed while fixing herself another drink."

"You better train your bitch to heel better," Shanice snapped. "You a dog whisperer, right?"

"Oh – is that why you have that collar around your neck? Besides, you just mad that he didn't want your stank ass pussy," Mesha teased.

Before she could get another sentence out, Shanice reached around Lucci and smacked Mesha in the mouth with the back of her hand like a mother would discipline a child. Pressing her head back she said, "Watch your mouth when you talking to grown folks, little girl. You better get something on your mind because what you're asking for is an ass whooping."

"No, that old bitch didn't," Mesha fumes as she rubbed her lips.

"Let's be real, I may have you by a year or two, but your hands tell the tale honey. You may want to try moisturizer. Now, I would advise you to back the fuck up, little girl, and take several seats. You can't hide behind the phone, or Lucci for that matter, now," Shanice answered.

Mesha sat her drink down and said, "Oh so you want to steal a bitch, right?" She then reached over Lucci's shoulder and connected with Shanice's jaw. Mesha rocked Shanice with the punch.

Moving her jaw around to test it for soreness, Shanice looked at Lucci and said calmly, "Move Lucci. It's time this little girl received the old ass whooping she's been asking for." Lucci, seeing the look of conviction in Shanice's eyes, moved out of the way.

Shanice rushed Mesha who, like the typical girl, went for the hair. Mesha couldn't get a grip, so when she tried a direct punch it just glanced off her ear. Shanice kept her momentum going and scooped Mesha up, slamming her on the floor. Scrambling to her knees, she then sat on top of Mesha's hips and began to throw punches connecting to her face. Every punch was accentuated with a word of warning: "I tried to tell you" – smack, "that you didn't want this old ass whopping" – smack, "but you didn't listen" – smack. "The next time" – smack, "grown folks are talking" – smack; "I bet that ass will be quiet" – smack, smack, and smack!

Lucci, having seen enough, pulled Shanice off Mesha who was at this point just trying to cover her face. "Y'all need to break this shit up," Lucci yelled pushing Shanice gently towards the door.

"You better be glad I slipped, or I would've had your old ass," Mesha yelled as she scrambled off the floor.

"You mean slip like that wig you got on? Motherfucker, please! You are as dumb as a box of rocks. Thanks for the cardio though. Girl, you wearing that old ass whooping," Shanice said sweetly as she walked towards the door, rolling her eyes when she reached Lucci.

"Keep rolling your eyes at me. I will shut them bastards for good," Mesha snapped. "Lucci move, let me two-piece this bitch," Mesha snapped.

"I thought you had on a three-piece lace front," Shanice asked as if she was concerned. "Oh, here's the third," pitching a track she had pulled out during the tussle. "You may want to try a new weaveologist as your hair game is weak."

Trying to keep a straight face, Lucci said, "Mesha, take the L. Y'all ain't about to tear up my shit."

"So, you on her side, Lucci?" Mesha asked.

"Listen, you got your ass beat fair and square. Don't be mad, just take it as a lesson learned," Lucci snapped. Lucci figured everything was done, so he moved out of the way. Just as he moved out of the way, Shanice gave Mesha a straight jab to the mouth.

"What the?" Mesha yelled, grabbing her bleeding lip.

Shanice made her way to the door then she turned around and said, "Now, we're done. Bye, Felicia! Enjoy."

Mesha regained her composure and said, "I'm going to get that bitch." She ran to the door and saw Shanice as she was getting in her car and said, "I got you, old bat, remember that," Mesha yelled.

Shanice just threw Mesha the deuces. "Whatever. Tootles," she yelled as she pulled off. Mesha walked back into the condo to find Lucci in tears laughing.

"What the hell is so funny?" Mesha fumed.

Lucci continued chuckling as he pulled at the blunt, and then pointed to Mesha, "You got knocked the fuck out."

"Tell that old bird I got her number," Mesha said as she reached for the blunt.

"Listen, if I were you, I would chalk it up as a loss and let it be," Lucci said as he passed the blunt.

"Oh, so you got jokes, right?" Mesha responded as she pulled on the blunt and exhaled.

Lucci burst out in laughter as he mimicked the punch

Mesha took to the mouth. Seeing the frustrated expression on Mesha's face as she walked past him, Lucci was taken aback as he responded, "Woo, hold up, Shorty. I have kept it one hundred. So, what you jealous?" he asked surprised. Just then the phone rang and Lucci answered as if Mesha didn't exist.

Mesha was quiet for a second then said, "Well, I see you're busy. Let me go before I say something I will regret later."

Not even acknowledging her comment, Lucci responded to the person on the other end of the line saying, "Do you want me to get rid of my company?"

Noticing Mesha had left the room and not quite trusting her in the house, Lucci made his way back into the living room with Mesha.

"You're a sorry ass host," Mesha snapped.

"Hey, listen, you were not invited so be thankful that I was hospitable," he teased. Mesha rolled her eyes and sucked her teeth.

"Tell you what, I'll let you make it up to me," Lucci responded. "But not tonight," he ended with a laugh.

His statement pissed Mesha off. "Why not tonight?" Mesha asked.

"Because I have something to do," Lucci answered.

"So, you're going to take a pass on this pussy?" Mesha asked looking at him like he lost his mind. Mesha's pussy was always wet in anticipation of putting in work with Lucci, but tonight with all the other crap from Shanice, this was really pissing her off.

"Yeah, not really in the mood. But listen you need to

bounce. Rain check?" Lucci fired up a blunt as he waited for Mesha to leave.

"Hey, Lucci? Lose my number," Mesha snapped as she grabbed her purse. Walking towards the door she purposely knocked over an expensive vase on a pedestal.

"Man, just let me see your head get small," Lucci laughed. This thing with Mesha was getting old anyway. She brought nothing to the table but greed, and to be honest she didn't challenge him mentally in the least. The sex was good, but he could get better.

Inhaling, he let the prime Kush absorb into his space. He was getting too old for this shit. He couldn't live in this fast lane long. Shanice's face had been in heavy rotation lately. He couldn't seem to get enough of her, though he would never tell her that. He was in such a relaxed state thinking about Shanice that he didn't realize that Mesha was still in the house.

"You full of shit, you know that, right?" Mesha countered.

As if seeing her for the first time he said, "I thought you were gone. Why are you still talking instead of walking?"

Guiding her to the door to make sure she left this time, Lucci kept a firm grip on her elbow. Mesha tried to slam the door, but Lucci caught the door and shut it gently. Mesha was salty about how Lucci treated her, but little did he know, she had something in store for his ass.

"Why do motherfuckers always want to tear up somebody shit," Lucci muttered to himself. He pulled out his cell phone and dialed Shanice's number. "Where are you?" Lucci asked.

"I'm at home. I can't do you anymore tonight."

"I just wanted to make sure you made it safely. Have a good evening, and I'll call you tomorrow." Shanice didn't have the energy to respond so she just hung up.

***

Still pissed off about what happened at Lucci's house, Shanice couldn't sit still, and she was nauseous. For weeks now she had been showing subtle signs of pregnancy, but this couldn't possibly be happening right now. She had only talked to Zeneka, but in her mind, she knew the pregnancy was real. Her biggest doubt was whether Lucci was ready to be a father.

She had always wanted children, but she had planned to be married and at a good place in her practice. Shanice had PCOS and though she could stand to lose a few pounds, her periods were never regular. Being the planner that she was, she had talked to her OB/GYN about what she would need to do to get pregnant, and he suggested Clonidine to not only regulate her periods, but also to make sure that she ovulated. She had done none of that and here she was – pregnant.

Though she had other prospects, she and Lucci had been on again, off again for a minute. She never thought it would develop into an emotional connection, let alone her getting pregnant. She was wrong on both counts. Why else would she be throwing blows? Thank goodness, her offense was on point or she could have gotten punched in the stomach. That would've been devastating in more ways than one.

She knew that Lucci was not the "settling down" type, and

honestly, that was what drew her to him in the first place. There were no strings attached, and he was an excellent lover. Shanice just never thought she'd find herself in this place. In Shanice's mind, while she never doubted that Lucci would take care of their child, she had no delusions about him staying with her exclusively.

It was too much to take in, and it wasn't going to be solved in the next five minutes, so Shanice set the alarms on her house and went to bed.

Chapter Ten
SAME STORM DIFFERENT DAY

The next day, Shanice was typing as Mitchell entered her office. "Good morning, Ms. Montgomery," he remarked to get her attention.

Shanice whipped around in her chair, still tired from the night before and really not in the mood for foolishness, didn't even lift her eyes from the file she was reading. "How can I help you?" she said with feigned indifference.

Mitchell nonchalantly answered, "Is this how you always handle business?" He knew his coy response was going to piss her off, but he liked it when she got angry.

Shanice, not willing to take the bait he was dangling, again responded, "How can I help you?" She continued working on her docket as if she were the only person in the room.

Mitchell just looked at Shanice with a cocky smirk on his face as he stepped back and said, "This is business.

Let the petty, personal shit go. I'm the new security liaison for David Alexander and Associates. Can you bring me up to speed with the Hobson case you're handling?"

Shanice rolled her eyes and responded, "I'm aware of your new role. Congrats, I think? As far as the case is concerned, that's something, as you know, that my paralegal could have provided, but I anticipated that you would ask, so I had her create one and place it in the file. The file is at her desk. Please close the door on your way out." Acting as if he was no longer in the room, Shanice went back to looking through her docket.

Mitchell, determined to sour her day, responded, "I will be the person that you're dealing with from now on," he answered boastfully. "Will that be a problem, Ms. Montgomery?" he asked contrarily.

Shanice paused for a moment and thought to herself, *"So this motherfucker wants to be brand new."* Putting her game face on, Shanice replied, "No, I look forward to working with you, Mr. Revis. Is there anything else I can do for you? I was in the middle of something."

Her demeanor took Mitchell aback. She treated him like a piece of gum stuck to the bottom of her shoe. "I guess that will be all for now," he responded.

Being in a spiteful mood Shanice snapped, "Please inform Mr. Montgomery that I really liked the flowers." Shanice knew that would get a rise out of him. She struggled not to laugh at his expression.

Mitchell was pissed at this revelation. "Excuse me?" he asked.

"Let Ted know that I appreciated the flowers," she said sweetly. Mitchell's whole demeanor changed as he answered. "Do I look like a fucking messenger?"

"Security liaison, messenger, all sounds the same to me," she joked, knowing that she had deflated his massive ego.

At that point, he was so mad he wouldn't have spit on Shanice if she were on fire. Without another word being said, he turned and walked out the door mumbling under his breath, *"Whatever, wait on that shit to roll off my tongue."*

Shanice just chuckled as his face told how he felt about her accusations. "You have a good day, Mr. Revis," she responded to the back of his head as he walked out the door.

And you can go fuck yourself, Shanice thought to herself. Not lying down with that man was the best decision she ever made. He was so aggravating and pompous that it grated on her nerves like chalk on a blackboard.

Chapter Eleven
MENDING FENCES

Zeneka's mind was still spinning about Jamari and all his fineness. She had almost forgotten that Meech was due home today. She made the phone call to Meech telling him what she felt, now it was time to follow through with the motions.

Parking her car in the drive, Zeneka hopped out to gather her backpack and purse. The front door was already open, and she could see Meech sitting in the family room watching television. He was still beautiful to Zeneka despite his many infidelities. She would always love him, but she was no longer in love with him. She didn't want this to be messy, so she decided to put her big girl panties on and come to him as a woman. If he chose to go sideways with it, then gloves off.

She made as much noise as possible when she entered the

house. Walking into the family room she greeted him saying, "Hey, Meech! How was your trip?"

"It was good," he said calmly. "Met some new contacts that may shake out in the future for Barksdale Corp. I've been waiting on you so that we can talk."

"Let me put my stuff down and fix a cup of coffee, and I'll meet you in the kitchen," Zeneka said with a half-smile. Meech stood to follow her to the kitchen. Zeneka pulled a letter-sized envelope out of the desk in the office and brought it with her when she returned to the kitchen. Meech had grabbed a Budweiser from the fridge and sat waiting patiently for her return.

Passing by the butcher-block Zeneka had a flashback of her night with Rozay that gave her body a hot flash. Noticing her hesitation, Meech asked, "Is everything alright?"

Zeneka shook her head as if she was knocking out cobwebs and went over to her Keurig to start her coffee. She grabbed the full mug and a can of milk from the fridge to use as a creamer. It was the way her G-mama taught her to make coffee, canned milk – Carnation if you got it, but Pet will do. There was already a container for sugar. Spooning in two tablespoons, she slid the document over to Meech for review.

Meech looked at the envelope for a minute before he opened it. This was really happening. He never thought that he and Zeneka would be talking divorce, but here they were, and it was all his fault. Clearing his throat, he opened the document and began to read through the Divorce Agreement. It laid out the properties in both North Carolina and the beach house in South Carolina. Zeneka wanted the beach house in Baldhead Island and offered him the house they had in North Myrtle. According to the document, they both agreed to forfeit rights to each other's retirement. Zeneka didn't want alimony but requested that he continue to make payments on their main home until she could get the house refinanced. Everything that she asked for was fair. She basically split all of their assets. After what he put her through, she was actually being more than fair.

Zeneka interrupted his thoughts when she said, "I figured we could have Shanice handle the arrangements. She actually drew up the document that you're looking at now. I understand if you feel more comfortable with getting your own attorney."

Clearing his throat again Meech said, "No, what you did seems fair, plus, she's my family attorney. Just let me know when I need to show up at Shanice's firm. In the meantime, I'm going to stay at the rental we have out at Coddle Creek. I'll need a few weeks to get it together because the renters left the house in a mess."

"That's cool. I'm in no hurry for you to leave. We can be adults and cohabitate until you have everything that you need," Zeneka said sincerely.

"For what it's worth, I really did love you, and I truly am sorry," Meech said looking at Zeneka intently.

Zeneka had a small smile on her face and tears in her eyes when she responded, "I have loved you for as long as I can remember. You were at one time all that I needed in this world. I wanted our relationship to be as happy and special as my parents'." One tear slid down her face as she continued on, "You were supposed to be my knight in shining armor, but I guess I was living in a world of fairy tales. I don't hate you, but the way you treated me has taken a lot out of me. I wish you nothing but the best, and I hope that you eventually find what it is that you were looking for." With that said, Zeneka stood up and gave Meech the sweetest kiss on his forehead and left the room.

Chapter Twelve
TIME TO MAKE THE DOUGHNUTS

Lucci sat back in the recliner and lit a blunt. As he sat meditating, there was a knock at the door. "Who is it?" he yelled.

"It's Mesha," she answered.

Lucci made his way to the door and opened it. "Wassup?" he asked.

"Nothing, was on this side of town, thought I would stop by," she replied.

Lucci responded, "Listen, this ain't that type of party." Mesha was wearing a low-cut top with a pair of jean shorts that accented her ass. Lucci was eyeing her from head to toe.

"So, what you got in mind?" he asked.

Mesha smiled and said, "Whatever you want."

"Oh, so it's like that?" he smiled while pulling on the blunt.

Mesha pushed her way past him. Lucci was in conflict because he knew that Shanice was the one he wanted, but his second brain was distorting his mental process. About five minutes later his cell phone rang, and he answered it. Mesha was always game for anything, and Lucci liked that about her, but he really didn't respect her for the same reason.

***

Lucci was sitting on the side of the bed smoking a blunt as the sun peeked through the blinds. It had been a couple of weeks since the epic beat down that Mesha took from Shanice. And just like Lucci knew that the sun would rise in the morning, he knew that Mesha would be calling him back for a hookup. She was one of those women that wanted to be kept, really didn't put anything into the relationship, but was always waiting with her hand out.

Eventually, he would need to cut her loose, but he wanted to get one for the road. Plus, Shanice was avoiding him. He thought that after a few days post "Rumble in the Jungle" she would've returned his call. If he was honest with himself, it was Shanice that he craved. She was like a well full of sweet water and he couldn't help but come back again and again to taste her sweetness.

"Time to make the doughnuts," he murmured to himself as he took in Mesha as she laid asleep. It was a phrase he and his brother used from an old Dunkin Doughnuts commercial. His mother always said that the early bird catches the worm, and don't burn the day.

Lucci still couldn't pinpoint what about this woman

turned him on. Maybe it was the ease of access. Whatever it was, it wasn't enough to sustain him. He was at that point in his life that he needed more than just a twenty-minute lay, no matter how good the lay was. Shanice's face kept popping up in his mind.

Thirty-minutes later, Mesha was waking up from the noise Lucci was making while he was piecing together his wardrobe for the day.

"Kill all that noise. I'm trying to get some sleep," Mesha snapped as she pulled the covers over her head. The pungent smell of marijuana invaded the room.

"Man, it's a new day," Lucci answered. "What? You going to sleep it away?" he asked.

Mesha peeked from under the covers and still pissed about the drama from a couple of weeks ago responded, "Too damn early to be that happy and to smoke weed."

Lucci just laughed, "It's never too early to burn trees. Plus, they are better than incense."

Lucci continued what he was doing. Mesha was aggravated by the noise he was making. "C'mon, baby girl, it's a new day," Lucci joked. "Let's get it popping. Are you hungry?"

Mesha knew he wasn't going to let her go back to sleep, so she sat up in the bed. "That weed has really jacked your filters up," Mesha growled as she stretched and yawned.

"No, I smoke it for clarity," Lucci interjected.

"Whatever, just let me get some sleep, and I will be good."

"C'mon now. Should have *taken* your ass to bed," he joked as he pulled on the covers. "Let's go get some breakfast and go from there." Lucci was bopping around the room after he pieced together his wardrobe.

"Lucci give me like three more hours of sleep, and I will be game for whatever," she responded.

***

It had been several weeks with no period, so for sure, Shanice was pregnant. Shanice had been avoiding Lucci like the plague partly because she was mad about Mesha being in his spot, but mostly because – well she just didn't know how to explain to him she was pregnant. They had only had sex a few times, but he must be fertile as hell.

She had to begin putting her affairs in order, and the first was informing Lucci of the new bundle of joy that would be arriving in seven more months, that is as soon as she got her courage up. Shanice was not afraid of her future; she was for once happy about the possibilities. What she was afraid of was a miscarriage. Her mother had difficulty carrying her and her brother. Shanice just prayed that legacy didn't pass on to her.

Jamari had been a Godsend. He was a good shoulder to cry on when she needed him, although she thought that there would be more going on with him and Zeneka. If there was, neither was talking. Zeneka seemed to be holding up well considering Meech did a one-eighty and was open about them separating and an amicable divorce. Shanice was happy for her because she had seen some nasty breakups both emotionally and financially and didn't want that for her girl.

Flipping through the files on her desk, she noticed a note

marked as urgent. It was from Mitchell – again. He was beginning to be a problem. She met Mitchell a few years back at a conference on cyber security and how firms should be looking out for this new threat. Mitchell was actually one of the presenters at the conference. He was a sharp cookie and not hard on the eyes either, and that's where it went south. He thought he was the smartest person in any room he stepped in. No one was allowed to have an opposing opinion. One dinner date was plenty to know that if she didn't cut the meal short, she was liable to choke the shit out of him.

Apparently, he didn't take rejection too well. Who relocates to a new state because they wanted a relationship with someone that they went on one dinner date, and then called maybe twice, and that was being generous? He was creepy and that was being polite. She had bigger fish to fry than Mitchell's foolishness, plus today, it wasn't worth the energy.

She made her way to her assistant's office. "Good morning," Shanice chimed. "What is the status of the Alexander case?"

"Well, we are waiting on Mrs. Alexander to return from her business trip, then she will be served," the petite woman answered.

"What about the Stratus settlement?" Shanice inquired.

Her assistant shuffled through the stack of files that were sitting on her desk. "We made them an offer, but their counter came in lower than expected," she answered.

Shanice was instantly aggravated by the response. "So, has anyone touched bases with them?" she asked.

"Yes, ma'am. Lieberman is right on top of it," she countered.

"Well, sometime today I need you to get a status report from him," she responded as she exited the office.

"I'm on top of it," she answered.

Ten minutes later, after making her daily rounds, Shanice was back in her office when her phone rang.

"Hello, Shanice Montgomery, how may I help you?"

"This is Zeneka. Are you busy?" Zeneka asked.

"Naw, wassup? So, long time no hear from you," Shanice replied.

Zeneka paused after the comment. "Nothing specific, just calling to connect. The last time we spoke, the conversation didn't end right. I miss my friend," she answered.

"So, where have you been?" Shanice inquired.

"I have just been chilling. You know, just living," she answered.

"Did you get that promotion?" Shanice asked.

"I haven't heard anything yet," she answered.

"So, how is little man?" Shanice asked.

"He's fine just growing every day," Zeneka replied. "I know what you're going to ask, and no, I haven't told her yet. I wanted to wait until the separation was finalized before I hit her with the news."

"You know, secrets have a way of eating away at you. They're like a wound that festers. If you don't take care of it, eventually it will take care of you," Shanice said thinking of her current situation. They were both quiet on the line, reflecting on what Shanice had just said.

"So, how are things at the office?" Zeneka asked.

"Don't get me started. You remember that dude Mitchell I met at the conference on cyber security? Well, he somehow made his way to North Carolina and is now working at my firm. Please don't get me started on that motherfucker girl," Shanice remarked.

"So, what did he do?" Zeneka asked.

"Nothing worth talking about," Shanice said.

Zeneka sucked her teeth and said, "Girl, we can roll up on his ass and fuck him up."

Shanice laughed and said, "Girl you know your ass is crazy, right?"

"Whatever, I'm just tired of them sorry motherfuckers," Zeneka responded, clearly irritated.

"So, have you talked to Zania?" Zeneka asked.

Shanice paused and answered, "I went by to check on her the day Meech moved into an apartment his family owns until his house is ready. She seemed like she was at peace with the decisions they are making."

"Ever thought that maybe she is just tired of his shit?" Zeneka snapped.

Shanice replied cryptically, "Well, you should know."

***

Meech felt like he was waking up when he felt the warmness of Neeka's mouth.

"Oh shit," he moaned. She worked her tongue from top to bottom. Her tongue sent chills up the base of his dick. He grabbed her by the back of her head as she bobbed and attempted to deep throat all nine inches. Saliva covered his dick while she stroked it slowly and talked to him.

"Damn, you feel so good in my hand," she moaned as Meech moaned in delight.

"Baby, this shit feels so good," he whimpered.

"You like that, huh?" Neeka eased her grip as she massaged the head of his dick.

"OOOO, ooo damn, that feels good. Don't stop, please. Uhhh," he whispered.

Neeka massaged his manhood as he wiggled from pleasure. "That's it baby, cum for mommy," she seductively whispered as she felt him stiffen in her hand. "You know what I want. Give it to me," she moaned as her strokes sped up.

"Damn, don't know what I did to deserve this, but thank you," he whispered.

Five minutes later, he was at the height of pleasure and he exploded. Meech couldn't remember the last time he came that hard. He writhed in pleasure. "Hot damn, hot damn," he repeated while she stroked him more firmly making him arch his back.

"You look beautiful in ecstasy," she whispered. As he laid back, she leaned forward and whispered in his ear, "So thick. I could rub your body all night," she breathed as she rubbed her hands down his thighs.

"I'm tired. Want to take a nap with me?" he responded.

Neeka compassionately responded, "Anything you want baby," as she laid her head on his chest.

The alarm clock began to buzz. He was now sweating and

twisted in sheets that were wet, extremely wet, and his hand gripping his dick. An event like this hadn't happened since he was in the ninth grade and had a massive crush on Sabrina Mitchell.

Talk about missed opportunities. Neeka was on his mind constantly. For him, this was a first because he never slept with her, yet they shared something more finite – intimacy. Looking at the sheets, it was obvious that he wanted her, but he had to come to her as a man. Right now, his life was a mess. When he returned from Savanah, he and Zeneka did something they hadn't done in years, sat down and had an intelligent conversation. It was a hard one because they were both honest about where they were emotionally.

He moved in a family spot out by the reservoir at Coddle Creek on the outskirts of Kannapolis and had been there for about two weeks. It was a two-story house that was built in the Charleston Antebellum style with decks on both levels of the house. The decks in this instance actually faced the lake. Though mostly wooded, the lot was cleared off so that you had an unobstructed view of the lake. In the mornings, we would sit out with a cup of coffee and just watch the water.

Life had a funny way of showing you what you really deserve. The only person that had been loyal to him, and thought he loved, was asking for a divorce. Though he had been fucking anything that moved for years, he found a woman that he hadn't touched yet. That was mindboggling for him. One thing was for sure, the more he abstained from sex, the clearer his mind became. It was almost like he was using sex to mask the pain of something. The more he thought about it, the sadder he got. To lift his spirits, he texted the person that had been in his dreams. His biological father, Vincent Barksdale, was always gone. He knew his namesake, but he only had a relationship with his grandmother, Sadie, uncles, and cousins. Vincent was always abroad for family business. His mother married a man who wasn't faithful or much for raising someone else's kids. So, that was the example set for him being a man. Vincent gave them a good life but wasn't one for long term commitment.

***

Lucci was freshly showered and dressed. He wasn't one for just lying around all day. Too much business can be missed that way. Even though he worked for the family, he still didn't get any breaks.

"Mesha, wassup? Are you rolling or what?" All Lucci heard was silence as he made his way into the bedroom. "Hey kid, you rolling or what?" Mesha didn't answer.

Lucci knelt down on the side of the bed and shook her. Half sleep, Mesha answered, "What's wrong?"

Lucci asked, "Are you okay?"

Mesha answered, "Just tired from last night."

Lucci shook his head and said, "You not used to running with the big dogs." Lucci stood up looking down at Mesha and asked, "Want me to bring you some food back?"

Mesha was nodding off as he talked.

"Well, I'm about to make my rounds, and I will be back," Lucci said.

Mesha sat up and said, "Listen this weekend was cool, but I ain't looking for nothing heavy right now."

Lucci just answered, "Not sure what gave you the impression that I was either. That's cool with me. I'm sure our paths will cross. Just lock up when you leave."

Mesha was shocked by his response. Lucci made his way out of the room towards the door when he heard footsteps behind him. He turned quickly.

"Wassup, shorty?" Lucci asked.

"I thought you were going to get some food and bounce," Mesha answered, "So, it's like that?"

"What? You thought I was going to fall apart because of what you said," he asked.

Mesha was offended and said, "It is what it is. You do what's best for you," Mesha snapped. "Just know you can't play me like one of your trick ass hoes."

"Listen, if it walks like a duck and quacks like a duck, it's a duck, right," Lucci answered nonchalantly.

Pissed off, Mesha stormed down the hall. Since she was acting all new, Lucci decided to make sure she was out of his house before he left. He didn't have a good vibe about Mesha. She was one of those messy types, and quite frankly Lucci was tired of buying new art pieces.

***

Thirty-minutes later, with Mesha out the house, Lucci felt like a cloud had lifted. While checking his watch for the time, he felt his phone vibrate and made his way to his car.

"Wassup? This Lucci," he answered.

"Well, it's my day off. Figured I would pamper myself by getting my hair done," Shanice said.

"Do you need some bread for that?" Lucci asked.

Mesha was calling Lucci phone as the conversation went on, but he just let her call go to voicemail. He was really vibing with Shanice, and nobody was going to distract him. They talked for hours. Shanice had his full attention. He knew he would have to be real because he could tell she wouldn't have it any other way.

"So, can I call you right back?" Lucci asked.

"Yeah, I would like that," Shanice answered.

After he had ended the call with Shanice, he returned Mesha's call. "Wassup," Lucci asked.

Mesha answered, "So, how long will you be out?"

Lucci answered, "I thought you told me to lose your number? Look, Mesha, we had fun, and now it's over. I don't want to have to block you from my phone. You have a good day." Lucci hung up the phone.

Mesha paused in disbelief. Never had she been shut down like that. This man must think she boo-boo-the-fool if he thinks she's going to be disrespected like she was some random thot. Mesha said to herself, *I got something for that ass! This motherfucker on some bullshit, tripping on a bitch. Let me hit up my brother and his jack boy squad.* She pulled out her phone to call her brother, Luda. Luda ran a clique of hittas who robbed drug dealers. He was known for his boldness, and he would post up their licks on social media. Luda's name brought fear to most d-boys and hustlers. "Wassup, bruh I got a lick for you up here," Mesha said as soon as he answered.

"What kind of numbers you talking?" he asked.

"Numbers where you can lay up for a while," Mesha confessed.

"Who is the mark?" asked.

"His name Lucci. He low-key, but he pushing numbers, has mob ties," encouraged Mesha.

"Sound like he needs me and the squad in his life," Luda laughed. "Aight, sis let me tie up some loose ends and I'm on that."

If I can't have his ass, the next bitch won't have him either, Mesha thought to herself. Mesha wasn't going to let Lucci get away with what she thought was disrespect, but in her heart, she knew that Lucci was in love with Shanice. She knew that setting Lucci up wasn't going to end well for her brother, Luda. Mesha just wrote it off as Luda knew his lifestyle came with hazards. She didn't want any of the money. She just wanted that to be Lucci's karma for playing her. "I knew you would be game for this lick," boasted Mesha.

"So how you know this nigga pockets inflated?" questioned Luda.

Mesha then answered, "Well, from what I've learned from the streets. Plus, being around him, he and his family have limitless money."

Luda was all ears at her words. "So, this dude got all this money, no one ever rolled his ass?" Luda questioned.

"Not that I know of," she responded. "Well, I will help. Give me a few days," Luda confirmed.

"Ok, hit me up when you touch down," Mesha said.

"One," Luda replied as he ended the call.

Mesha smiled to herself. She and Cashmere had set plenty of ballers up who had pissed them off. In her eyes, she felt that Lucci had led her on, and she wanted him to feel her pain.

Chapter Thirteen
SOMETHING NEW

Lucci and Shanice had been talking on the phone constantly for days. He was just getting back from his trip, and the only thing on his mind was hearing Shanice's voice. Confused about what he was feeling, he decided to check on his brother to see how he was holding up.

"Wassup, bro what's good," he said when Meech answered.

"Wassup, big bruh. You getting settled at your new spot?" Lucci asked.

"No, not yet. I'm crashing at Zeneka's still," Meech answered.

"It's different not seeing Zeneka when I get home from work because she's the social butterfly now," Meech said sounding off in Lucci's ears.

"I heard from Shanice that she be out getting turned up," Lucci answered. "So how are y'all getting along?"

"We maintaining," Meech retorted. "You never miss your water until your well runs dry."

"Shit!" Lucci said. "That bad bruh? 'Cause you pumping a dry well with Zeneka."

"Yeah, I fucked that up," Meech sighed.

He could tell he was at work by the noise in the background. "Is this a bad time for you?" Lucci asked.

"Well, I was in the middle of something, but I'm glad that I was on your mind," Meech answered. "Think I'm about to shut it down for the day. Hey? When is the last time you talked to Absalom?"

"Is he back? I thought he was in South Africa," Meech intervened.

"Talked to him earlier in the week. Why?" Lucci answered cryptically.

"Nothing, just wondering why I haven't heard from him," he answered.

"Have you told him you getting a divorce?" Lucci questioned.

"No, told you I haven't talked to him," Meech whined.

"Well, I schooled him when we talked. He just said he hope you're fair in the final settlement," Lucci added.

"I told you I'm going to do her right," Meech agreed. "No problem, bruh, he's family. If you talk to him again, tell him to hit me up."

"You know Absalom. He'll call you," Lucci ended with a laugh. "I'm up for a night of chilling. What are you up to?"

"Look, I'm about to shut down. Swing by the house tonight, and we'll catch a game. Bring some cold one's, I'm sure we will have the spot to ourselves," Meech confirmed. "I'm sure Zeneka will be at somebody's something."

"Role reversal is a bitch, huh, big bruh?" Lucci joked.

Zeneka kept herself busy by avoiding Meech because he still lived there while he waited on his new house. "Aight, bruh see you in a few," Meech said.

"One," Lucci said in response.

***

Meech, getting nothing done at work, decided to pack it up and continue to work from home. He was in his room preparing for a presentation the next day when the phone rang. "Hello," he answered.

"Do you know how much I miss your voice?" she asked.

Meech responded, "Yeah, glad you called. I almost forgot. Where are you at?"

"I'm just getting out of class. I should be home in about twenty minutes. I miss your face," Neeka answered.

Normally they would FaceTime, but since Neeka would have to drive soon, that would take place later that night. Meech was grinning from ear to ear when he heard a knock at the door. Meech asked, "Who is it?"

Lucci answered, "It's me."

Shit, he thought to himself. He didn't realize that it was that late. "Come in," he answered. Each brother had keys to each other's spot in case of emergency.

Lucci walked in wearing a black jogger and some retro red, black, and white Air Force Ones with a red Nike shirt.

"Hey, listen," Neeka started, "have you seen your girl?"

Meech answered, "Naw, I haven't seen her since I returned from Savanah. She must be traveling. Why, wassup?"

Neeka was quiet for a minute, and then she said, "Well, I saw her stud friend, Sweets, in the hotel bar."

Meech looked puzzled as Neeka told him the stud that Pleasure called Sweets had popped up in random places where she'd be. It was almost as if she was following her. After he spoke with Pleasure and before he left, he thought they were good. He'd have to call her and tell her to call off her pit bull.

Still not convinced that it was Pleasure's stud, Meech asked her again, "Are you sure it was her, Sweets?"

"Positive. There are some faces you don't forget, and hers is one of them," Neeka ended a little breathy.

"Are you at your car?" Meech didn't like when she had late, evening classes. It bothered him until he knew she was in her car safely. Meech was falling in love with Neeka, but with all the dirt he had done to Zeneka; he was waiting on karma, but he didn't want it to affect him and Neeka.

"Yep. I'm headed home. I will text you soon as I get into the door. Call you at eleven," Neeka said sweetly.

"Aight, Bae," Meech said and ended the call.

Lucci was looking at his brother with a curious expression on his face. Making his way to the wet bar off the family room

"Let me prove your ass wrong," he muttered to himself as he dialed Pleasure's number. After five rings, someone answered the phone.

"Hello," the voice answered.

Recognizing the voice, Meech was pissed when he asked, "Is this Pleasure Morris's phone? Who is this?" he snapped.

"She's in the shower," the person responded.

"Who the hell am I speaking too?" he snapped.

"Sweets," the voice answered. "She's in the shower. Would you like to leave a message?"

"Actually, you're the person I would like to speak to. I understand that you have been following my girl around, for that matter, I saw you a few times myself while I was in Savanah. Is there a problem?" he asked.

"I've checked you before about a bitch," Sweets snapped.

"He, she, whatever the fuck you are, back the fuck up off mine. That shit is creeping her the hell out," Meech spat.

Sweets laughed to herself flashing back to the hotel run-in they had.

Sucking his teeth Meech responded, "What you fake ass dudes don't understand is tongue and a rubber dick only goes so far. Homegirl, boy don't get mad at me cause plastic not working for her," Meech teased.

"Well, if that's the case, why you sweating it?" Sweets teased. "I love that fat ass she has. Besides, I don't think I've had Native American before. I definitely have that on my radar," Sweets said, wanting to antagonize Meech.

"I'm not the one you want to fuck with, homeboy. Fall

back," Meech fumed. "Barksdale's the last name. Check my resume, homeboy."

"Lil' boy, if I'm not a threat your punk ass wouldn't be calling me. I'm quite familiar with the Barksdale's. Get the fuck outta here with that shit. As much as I have enjoyed this conversation, I got to find your girl, or should I say our girl," Sweets laughed, hanging up before Meech could get a chance to say something.

"I see that I'm going to have to fuck this fake ass dude up," Meech fumed.

Meech hung up the phone and said, "Ain't that about a bitch."

Lucci looked at his brother concerned and asked, "Are you okay?"

Meech was still in a daze trying to sort out what was going on. "How the fuck did she know that Neeka had Native American ancestry?" Game recognized game and there was more to Sweets than what met the eye. She wasn't your everyday stud. Frustrated, but powerless, Meech said to himself, *For right now, fuck it.* He looked at Lucci and said, "Can you pour me a shot of that cherry moonshine?"

"Damn, bruh where you get this firewater?" Lucci questioned. "I need a blunt with that."

Lucci looked surprised because the only time 'shine was pulled out is when you were looking to hurt yourself or get turned up. That shit would put hair on your chest. It was straight from the hills of North Carolina.

Handing the glass to his brother he said, "And here I was

about to bounce some questions off you. Looks like someone got you twisted up in the game."

Taking the glass straight back, Lucci asked. "You still got Gotti number?"

"You talking about Aunt Hattie's grandson, right?" Meech replied.

"Yeah. I haven't seen him in a minute. Let me call Yella right quick. He should have it." Picking up the phone to dial Yella, that name kept rolling around in Lucci's head. Yella answered on the second ring.

"Wassup people, it's been a minute."

"Nothing much, you and Gotti were on my mind," Lucci interjected.

"We good up here folk, thanks to you," Yella laughed.

"Yep, just the usual. A few hating ass niggas, but other than that we good."

"What is Gotti up too? He's like family too," Lucci questioned.

"He around. You know his ass living that square life. Plus, he fucked up and got this psycho ass girl pregnant," Yella chimed.

"No shit, do you know her? So, he going through?" Lucci teased. "When you get a minute, tell him to hit me up, cuz. Well, I just wanted to check on y'all. We family, we got to do better," Lucci said.

"I agree cousin, but times fly when you chasing money. Trapping no excuse though," Yella agreed.

"Aight, cuzzo. We definitely got to do better. Remember

we're second generation Barksdales," Lucci confirmed as he ended the call.

Meech sipped on the shine and watched the game. "Bruh, I just touched bases with Yella. Same ol' shit. Different days." Lucci blurted.

"Oh okay, cool," a slightly buzzed Meech answered.

"We need to get up with them soon," Lucci responded. Meech just shook his head in agreeance as the 140-proof shine crept up on him.

"I'm about to step out and smoke me a blunt," Lucci cheesed.

"Okay, I'm on this shine, and K.D. getting off in these boys' asses," Meech chimed.

As Lucci stepped outside to go get his weed from the car, Zeneka was getting out of her car. Hoping that she wouldn't pop off, he spoke, "Wassup, Zeneka."

His salutations fell on deaf ears as she walked up the stairs to enter the house.

Zeneka walked into the living room then spat, "I see some shit don't change."

Meech, tipsy, was caught off guard by Zeneka. "Man, stay in your lane. We just chilling watching the game," Meech snapped back.

"Whatever, you will be gone soon enough," Zeneka hissed.

"Aight, take your ass upstairs or wherever you going. You don't want these troubles," Meech fumed as Zeneka walked upstairs. "My house ready so I will be gone tomorrow," Meech added.

Zeneka came back to the top of the stairs then responded, "Thank you, Lord. I'm fucking excited." "What the fuck ever," Meech spat as he heard the door slam.

Moments later, Lucci stuck his head in the screen door. "Bruh, wassup with your people? Zeneka is on one. You need to check her, but far as that other situation, don't sweat it."

"I'm not worried about Zeneka, but this Sweets chick, I am," he fussed.

"Did you say Sweets, bruh?" Lucci asked as he handed Meech the bottle of cherry shine. He looked like he needed another drink. "Bruh, she's a stud chick right," Lucci said as he reclined back.

"Yeah, that's the one that Pleasure's fucking. Her punk ass been fucking with Neeka's job," he answered.

Always the jokester of the two brothers, Lucci dropped all pretenses and said with a dead serious face, "Meech let that go. You don't need those troubles. She down with the family," Lucci explained. "I know her through me and Yella fucking with our cousin Damien."

"I don't give a fuck about all that. Sweets better step off my chick before I body her big ass," Meech fussed as he sipped in between.

"That's our folks, but I will go to war for you if she on some bullshit," Lucci assured Meech. "Forget all of this for a minute and focus on your pending divorce."

"Don't sweat that, little bro. I'm a Barksdale. We always come out on top," Meech grinned. "Plus, I'm giving her everything."

"That's fair. You really put her through, bruh," Lucci chimed.

Meech was shocked at Lucci's response. Usually, he was his biggest co-signer. "If that ain't the pot calling the kettle black," Meech joked.

Lucci shot him the side-eye then spat, "The difference is, I wasn't married or in a relationship, bruh."

Later the next day......

After his talk with Lucci, Meech felt like shit. He was sitting in the office thinking about their pending divorce. *"Damn, I fucked up,"* he muttered to himself.

He saw the toll cheating could take on a person through the eyes of his mother. He rubbed his hand over his head aggravated to see that Lucci had hung up his player's card and was in love with Shanice. In a sense, he felt like he was losing his brother and partner in crime. He was feeling like his world was caving in on him because, in a span of two months, he was ending his marriage, and Lucci was in love with Shanice. He was jealous, but happy for him. He knew that he hadn't done right by Zeneka, even though he knew she had stepped out on the marriage with Rozay.

"I'm definitely going to get with his ass," he growled as he slammed his fist on the desk. "That motherfucker bold enough to touch what's mine."

Meech had someone tailing him for a week, tapping his phone. He knew that Rozay was meeting Zeneka, so he was definitely going to settle the score today. Just as he was about to explode Vincent walked in.

"You got a minute?" Vincent inquired.

Meech, still pissed, answered, "Sure, what's up?" Meech and Lucci never really had a relationship with Vincent. Their Uncle Absalom was more of a father figure because Vincent was too selfish to be a father, but he was a great provider. They never called him Dad, but out of respect for Absalom, they were always respectful of him.

"Hey, listen. I know this talk is a little too late, but Zeneka is truly her name," Vincent advised. "Don't be me. I regret every day I didn't wife your mother."

Meech's head dropped because Vincent had just dropped a gem. "So, now you're a philosopher and father now?" Meech asked, already pissed. Vincent rubbed his hand across his face.

"Oh, believe me, I have a life of regrets from decisions I've made," Vincent responded.

"I wake up every day knowing that I'm just like you. That shit's like a curse," Meech fussed.

Vincent was hurt by Meech's scathing view of him, but this was long overdue.

"So, why is it your brother and family loved us, but you couldn't?" Meech questioned as tears of frustration streamed down his face.

Vincent stood up then responded, "You thought I didn't love y'all? What the fuck? I was running the family business. I never wanted this for y'all." He walked over to console him, but Meech extended his arm to rebuff him.

"I'm good on you. Save that," Meech fumed.

Vincent wasn't surprised by Meech's reaction. Trying to

stay intact he said, "Again, I'm sorry that my actions ruined your life."

"Save that shit. G*et* the fuck out of here," Meech yelled. "You need to be telling my mother this." Meech's words deflated Vincent, but he wasn't blind to his son's resentment towards him. He had no words as he exited Meech's office. Minutes later, Meech was ransacking his office. In the middle of his tirade, there was a knock at the door.

"Mr. Barksdale, are you okay?" his secretary, Margaret, asked.

Meech shot her a bewildered look and she closed his office door. As soon as she closed the door, he slid down the wall and wailed for what seemed like an hour as memories flooded his mental rolodex

He wanted to hate Vincent, but he couldn't. He knew, like himself, Vincent was a man who had made irreversible mistakes. He sobbed as he dialed his mother's number. It had been awhile since he talked to her, but he and Lucci had always taken care of her very well.

"Hello," his mother answered.

"How are you doing?" Meech pried.

"Who am I speaking too?" his mother asked.

"It's Meech, Ma," he answered.

His mother was in the early stages of Alzheimer's. "Meech doesn't live here," she confirmed.

Meech had heard from Lucci that her condition was getting worse. Silence fell as she kept saying hello. Meech ended the call. He was crushed that the woman who had always been independent and beautiful, was a shell of herself. He was cried out. He knew that he had a second chance with Neeka. A lot of Neeka's characteristics reminded him of his mother. As he was getting balanced, beating Rozay ass was the top of his agenda. It wasn't about Zeneka, it was the fact that Rozay was bold enough to fuck his wife in their house. Meech grabbed his briefcase as he exited his office. He stopped by Margaret's desk to tell her he would be gone the rest of the day.

****

It was late, too late, and Shanice was sitting in her office waiting on her assistant to bring her the latest indictments from the federal courts. There were three divisions of her firm: Family Law, Criminal Law, and Personal Injury – specifically medical malpractice. Each branch had its own suite of offices, and Shanice had cut her teeth in Criminal Law. Her specialty now was estates and trusts, along with complicated adoptions, and unfortunately messy divorces.

"Ms. Montgomery, the files you requested are now uploaded," her assistant said.

"Thank you," she responded.

As she was about to leave, she asked Shanice, "Ms. Montgomery, will there be anything else?"

"That will be all," Shanice answered as she picked up her phone to call Zeneka.

"Hello, this Zeneka," she answered.

"Hey, this is Shanice. Wassup?"

"Nothing much, just cleaning," she answered. "Aggravated

that I got home last night and Meech and Lucci were posted up at the house after I had a long day of work. I was kind of mean."

"Sooo, what happened that day? Did you see Rozay?" Shanice inquired.

After moments of silence Zeneka answered, "Yeah, I talked to him."

Shanice knew it was more to it. She blurted out, "OOO, you little whore. You fucked him again," she joked.

Zeneka just giggled. "I mean, we did talk, but it didn't lead to other things," she countered.

"So, have you all decided what you all are going to do?" Shanice inquired.

"We are definitely divorcing. We have grown apart, but I believe we're both glad it's over," Zeneka said.

Zeneka answered, "I gave him the paperwork you provided, and he's on board. Didn't even argue. Not sure what happened while he was in Savanah, but he's different."

Shanice said, "Well, you know I'm here if you need me. So, you are serious about this?"

Zeneka answered, "Yeah it has been a long time coming. I thought I would fall apart, but I'm relieved it's over. I asked God to move, so I can't be afraid to step when he opens the door."

"Girl, you want me to throw you a divorce party?" Shanice joked.

Zeneka laughed and said, "You know your ass is crazy, right?"

"So, I guess new dick gives you clarity?" Shanice teased.

"Have you talked to Zeneka? She's probably in the midst of some bullshit."

"No, she's been ghost lately. I'll call her tomorrow," Zeneka said, bending with a grunt picking up some clothes that fell to the floor.

Looking at the stack, she saw something that didn't belong. Meech had been moving some of his clothes, but she knew these boxers didn't belong to him.

Rozay, she thought. *That sneaky motherfucker.*

Hearing her grunt, Shanice knew something was wrong, "You good, girl?"

"Yeah, I just found something I didn't expect to find. Enough about me, how are you feeling? Has the morning sickness slowed down?" Zeneka asked concerned.

"I'm dealing with it," Shanice answered. "I'm still taking it all in."

Taking a closer look at the file that had come up with pending indictments, Shanice saw something that was not expected. "Hey, girl, I'm gonna have to hit you back. Something came up at work completely unexpected."

"No worries. I will holler at you this weekend," Zeneka said, who was now on ten with what she had found. There was a reason that she didn't commit to Rozay, and now the evidence was in her hands. He was petty and messy like a female. *I'm glad I swerved his ass,* she said to herself.

Disconnecting the call, Shanice took out her personal phone and looked for a number she hadn't called in at least ten years. She knew he'd answer because she too had the same number that she had ten years ago.

****

Sweets walked into the large bathroom to a freshly showered Pleasure who was putting coconut oil on her arms and legs. She was mid-bend when Sweets came from behind, spread her legs, and entered her from behind. Arguing always made her horny as hell, and her lil' boyfriend had a good clap back. Pleasure, always the one in control, came on mid-stroke. Sweets had made sure that her strap was fully lubricated because she wanted to please, not hurt. So, she did what she did best and went to work making little miss control freak bend over and touch her toes.

Pleasure had no idea what pissed Sweet's off, but she was thanking them silently. That bitch was putting it on her with no mercy. She hadn't had dick this good since, well, since the last time they were together. She laughed to herself. Hearing her giggle, Sweets slowed to slow, teasing strokes that she knew would have Pleasure in tears. She snatched her hair by the top knot she had pinned it up in.

Too many orgasms to count and an hour later, Pleasure sat in her room too tired to lift her head. Sweets looked like she could go another four hours.

Looking at her lover and touching her face she asked, "What the fuck got into you? I mean, I'm not complaining, but seriously what's up?"

Sweets was silent then said, "So, your man called?" with irritation in her voice.

Pleasure responded, "What man?"

"The little boy who was sweating you in Savanah. So, wassup?"

Looking confused, Pleasure asked, "What do you mean?"

"We have some unfinished business," Sweets responded.

Pleasure answered, "I'm not gay. I'm just curious."

Aggravated at the situation, Sweets snapped, "You are gay, you just haven't embraced it, yet."

Pleasure responded, "I'm not gay, like I said. Don't be kicking me that dumb shit."

"Don't get it fucked up. You going to get a motherfucker laid to rest on some bullshit," Sweets added as she lit a blunt.

They had made their way back to the bedroom and Sweets had dipped into the stash of Kush she kept at Pleasure's place.

Taking a drag from the fresh blunt she asked, "So, why the fuck was I eating your pussy for the last twenty minutes then?" Sweets asked.

Pleasure was quiet as the true depth of her actions had sat in.

"What? Cat got your tongue?" Sweets snapped. "Seriously, I didn't force you to do anything you didn't want to do."

Pleasure saw Sweet's point of view. Subconsciously, she had desired a woman, and maybe she was with a man because it was more accepting to society.

"So, what do you want from me?" Pleasure asked.

"I just want you to stop lying to yourself," Sweets answered. "So, can we finish our business?" she asked.

Pleasure then answered, "And what business is that?"

Flipping Pleasure on her stomach and dragging her to the end of the bed, Sweets said, "Sealing the deal of course. Obviously, you need more convincing on who this pussy belongs to, but I promise you that once I leave for my flight back to Vegas this afternoon, there will be no doubt."

Normally, Pleasure was the one who dominated in the bed, but there was something about Sweets that both made her cream and scared her at the same time. From her position on the bed, Pleasure faced the mirror. Looking up she had a full view of her on all fours, and Sweets lined up for entry into her already dripping pussy. The look on her face was one of both lust and possession, and quite frankly for the first time in a long-time, Pleasure was scared. Not scared that Sweets would hurt her physically, but more afraid that if she truly gave in to her feelings, Sweets would break her heart. All thoughts left her mind as soon as she stroked into her waiting pussy. *"Shit,"* she thought to herself as she moaned aloud. She had switched over to the ten-inch width.

Closing her eyes and enjoying the feeling, Sweets pulled her gently, but securely by her ponytail and said, "No, baby, I want you to watch me fuck this pussy into submission." With the first stroke, Pleasure screamed her name. Sweets replied, "The only thing that I want to hear from your lips is *it's mine*" Going deep, she commanded, "Say it!"

With an erotic scream, the orgasm was so intense that she had tears in her eyes. The look on Sweets face through the mirror made her body shake. It was then that she knew she was way over her head.

***

Shanice was sitting in her office when her paralegal, Carolyn, walked into her office with a copy of those getting charged with indictments. Shanice combed over the list, muttering names to herself, then dropped her head, "Oh shit! This is the last thing I need."

Carolyn gave her a confused look, "Is everything okay?"

Distracted, Shanice said, "Yes, Carolyn can you get Absalom Barksdale on the phone for me?"

Seeing the intense look on her face, Carolyn answered, "I'm on it boss."

Shanice read the charges. "Human Trafficking? What the fuck?" she sighed.

"Shanice, pick up. Mr. Barksdale is on the line."

"Well, hello young lady. It's been awhile," Absalom said.

"I know, I need to stay in touch. It has been awhile. Sorry to call at this late hour sir, but I have urgent news that I wanted to get to you as soon as possible. I hate to be the bearer of bad news," Shanice said.

"That's why you have my personal line in case of urgent situations. Now, tell me what has caught your attention," he asked smoothly.

"Indictments are out, and Anthony's name is on there," she responded.

"Under what charge? Can you divulge that information?" Absalom inquired.

"They are charging him with human trafficking, Absalom," she answered.

Shanice knew by Absalom's silence that the news was disappointing. Anthony Barksdale was heir to the Barksdale billions, but unfortunately, not the sharpest tool in the shed. Shanice had met the elder Barksdale while in college, and he was also Meech and Lucci's uncle. Shanice and Anthony actually attended law school together. He barely passed, and there was a rumor that some of his grades were literally paid for so that he could graduate.

From what she remembered of him in college, he was a loose cannon. Walking around like he owned the world with zero couth or swag. Now, his little brother Damien was another matter. He attended MIT. He was what she and Zeneka would term alpha, geek, intelligent, and sexy. If anybody should be running the Barksdale empire, it should be Damien.

"Thank you for the call, Shanice. I'll be in town in the next month or so. You and I will do lunch or dinner. I will not take no for an answer."

"Thank you, Absalom. I look forward to that. Is there anything that you want me to do with regards to the charges?" There were few people that Shanice would move heaven and earth for, and Absalom Barksdale was one of them.

Absalom was tired of his son's fuckups. "Well, let him take his licks. I've covered him long enough," Absalom grumbled. "Hard head makes a soft ass."

Shanice searched for the right words to say because Absalom was a close friend, more like family.

"I will put my team on it. Whatever he's doing, shut it down," Shanice said.

"Thank you, and consider it done," Absalom said as he ended the call.

Shanice called for Carolyn.

"What do you need?" Carolyn asked.

"Find out who our top attorneys are in the Nevada office, specifically those that specialize in immigration and human trafficking."

"I'll have a list of names for you by nine a.m. tomorrow morning," Carolyn replied. "I will pull the team together. I'm on it."

"Thank you, Carolyn. Will you pull my door, behind you?" Shanice smiled.

***

Zeneka was doing laundry and reminiscing about the time she had spent with Jamari at Edith's. They hadn't even kissed yet, and she was so caught up. When she saw him at school yesterday, they had set up a date for bowling. She hadn't gone bowling in years, so if nothing else it would be comical.

She was talking to Shanice and putting a load in the washer when she saw some turquoise boxers. Instantly pissed off, she said to herself, *What the fuck? I know this punk ass motherfucker didn't leave his drawers in my house.* She whipped out her cellphone and called Rozay. He picked up on the second ring.

"Wassup, sexy, I must've crossed your mind?" he boasted.

Zeneka had to pull her ear from the receiver and count to five. He was so unbelievably cocky.

"Excuse you. I see you on some petty shit like a salty ass chick," Zeneka fumed.

Rozay knew she had discovered the boxers he had stashed. "What did I do to you?" he joked.

"So, you gonna play dumb, right?" Zeneka asked. "So, what your ass thought that Meech was going to find them? Your buster ass is weak. I see you have bitch tendencies."

Rozay was getting tired of her verbal barrage and said, "I see you all on the weak ass nigga dick the other night, but you call me a lame?"

"You're married, but fucking me in your house," Rozay joked. "You come at me because you're in your feelings because you weren't ready save that bullshit."

Zeneka was caught off guard that Rozay was coming at her like that.

"Whatever, he's not a lame or thirsty like your ass. No, I'm not fucking with you. Like, I gave you the ass once. You tripping. If you were getting it on a regular, your ass would be gone over this goldmine," Zeneka laughed.

"Whatever, man, save that shit," Rozay sighed. "It wasn't the best I've had."

"Well, anyway, I just wanted to read your ass. Now it's time for me to get dressed to hang out with his lame ass. Deuces," Zeneka joked.

"HHHold up, your ass will get yours soon enough since you a bad bitch now," Rozay laughed hysterically before ending the call.

Zeneka began to rethink her security around the house.

Zeneka was pissed that she should have never given Rozay bitch ass her cookies. In hindsight, she did move too fast with him. She had flight of fancy that maybe he could be her prince charming, but that turned out to not be the case. He was just another egotistical man on the hunt for new ass. She laughed to herself because her lapse of bad judgment showed her that she was definitely going to go a different route with Jamari. "That bitch ass nigga," she muttered.

***

Meech was just getting out of the shower when he heard his cell chime. It had taken some time, but he had finally gotten settled in his new digs. He was drying off when the chime went to a ring. Looking at the caller ID he smiled and answered, "Hey, Bae! Wassup?" It was Neeka, and Meech had an instant hard-on at the sound of her voice.

She missed Meech so much. They had an intimate connection, and she really enjoyed sharing his mental space. They could talk about anything and everything. She really wanted to take the relationship to the next level. Her dad was a good reader of character, and she wanted to introduce him to Meech.

Since their son had recently moved to North Carolina they decided to check out the beach, see the place where flight first took place. They rented a house at Kitty Hawk and had invited their children out for the fourth. Neeka had never seen the coast of North Carolina and had heard a lot about the beauty of the beaches. From what she understood, it was not commercialized like some beaches, so some spans were semi-private. If things worked out well for the fourth, then she would invite him out to the ranch for Christmas. She was excited about the possibilities with Meech. Of course, he would need to stay in the bonus room because her parents were old school and didn't play that.

"Nothing, making sure you hadn't forgotten about me coming," she responded.

"No, baby I haven't forgotten. You ready to see a brother, huh?" Meech joked.

"Well, my parents and brother are ready to meet this mystery man," she giggled. "Plus, my brother invited his new girlfriend."

Meech was nervous about meeting Neeka's family. Most women he dealt with he did well to remember their name let alone meet their family.

"So, are you ready to see me?" Neeka questioned. "Did you get everything moved into your place, babe?"

"Yeah, I have a few more things to get, but overall, yes," Meech said. "Do we need to take anything to the picnic?" Meech asked in concern.

Neeka thought about it then joked, "Just your fine ass. I'm so ready to see you. I know we FaceTime, but I need to feel you next to me," she ended with a sigh. Meech just smiled because he truly loved Neeka, and he would do anything to make it work with her.

"I'm ready for you to move here," Meech answered.

"If you don't mind, I'd like to drive out to the Outer Banks versus fly. You get to see my beautiful state, and we can spend some time together before meeting your parents."

"That sounds like a plan. I love a good road trip," she said.

"Umm, sweetie? she asked hesitantly. "We'll need to sleep in separate bedrooms. As a matter of fact, I think I might be bunking with my brother's new boo. You and he will be sharing a room. My parents are very old school. I hope you don't mind."

Meech cleared his throat and said, "Not at all. I can respect that. I would rather make a good impression than a bad one."

"Thanks for understanding. Sooo babe, have you talked to your ex?" Neeka asked.

"Only when necessary. Bae, come on. She's not a threat to us. She's living her life. It's time for us to start living ours," Meech sighed, frustrated that he had to keep reassuring her about their relationship.

In a way, he couldn't blame her as his background wasn't exactly squeaky clean. He really wanted to do right by Neeka. Meech knew that he had fucked up royally in the past and was hoping to make this relationship right. "I'm all yours. She's dating, and we're just waiting on the paperwork," he said with confidence.

"I believe you, babe. I just really want us to work – no distractions. Look, they're calling for my zone for seating for the flight to Charlotte. See you at the airport when I touch down," Neeka said.

"Okay, babe. I will see you in a little while. Love you,"

Meech smiled. Neeka was caught off guard with his I love you.

"I love you too," Neeka stammered as she ended the call. She had just entered unchartered territory. He said it first, and she was on cloud nine. Neeka had been feeling it for a minute, and now that he said it, it made what she felt tangible.

Bringing storm clouds to her otherwise sunny day. "Why you telling this nigga you love him in my presence," Luda joked. "So, when you going to tell your boyfriend about me?" Luda smirked.

Neeka frowned at his statement then said, "Boy, bye! Save that shit for one of your birds. You've never touched this."

Luda moved in closer while she was talking and pressed his lips against hers. Neeka pushed him away at first, but when he cupped the back of her head and slipped his tongue in between her lips, all her fighting ended. To her dismay, she kissed him back. Maybe it was the absence of Meech, and she just wanted to be touched. Or maybe she had just lost her mind. Either way, she was saved by the bell. The announcement of their flight broke the kiss up.

"What the hell you doing?" Neeka snapped.

Luda smiled and said, "Don't play – you liked it," as he grabbed his bags and headed down the concourse.

Neeka felt like a thot because she had never been unfaithful to Meech. As far as she knew, he had been faithful to her. Hell, he was leaving his wife for her. She met Luda from growing up around each other and college. He was cool as hell and easy to talk to, plus he always made sure that she made it to her car safely when they left class. He was the perfect gentleman. Luda had always been like a big brother to her, but lately, he had been making it known that he wanted more. Neeka let him outpace her walking towards the flight because she knew she had to distance herself from him because her heart belonged exclusively to Meech.

"Quit tripping. Come on before you miss this flight," Luda said.

"Don't play me like that. You're like a brother to me," Neeka growled. He knew that he was wrong, but he knew she enjoyed the kiss regardless of what she said.

"Chill the hell out. It wasn't that serious," he frowned.

"So, are you following me?" Neeka asked.

Luda brushed her comment off then responded, "Don't gas yourself up like that. I'm going to see my damn sister." Luda shook his head realizing that he needed to fall back on any intent he had of him and Neeka.

"Keep lying to yourself," Neeka teased as she boarded the plane.

***

Later after his flight at Mesha's spot.......

Mesha picked Luda up at the airport. They were plotting on how he could pick Lucci off so she wouldn't be tied to it. At 6'4" it wasn't like Luda would be invisible. He had the build of a linebacker and with his line of work as a bodyguard at the hottest club in Savannah. He had to stay in top shape. Stepping out of the rental car with his low fade, he was decked out in stonewashed Levi's with the matching jacket, green Ralph Lauren hoodie, and wearing white K-Swiss.

Mesha was wearing a purple, fitted dress with black Louboutin's. Luda sparked up a blunt as they sipped on some Ace of Spades.

"Bruh, you got to time this shit right and disappear," Mesha said as she hit the blunt passing it back to Luda.

"Chill, sis, I got this. I'm a light his ass up like a Christmas tree, and I'm ghost," he joked.

"Aight, I just don't want it to fall back on my doorstep," Mesha snapped.

Her comments fell on deaf ears while Luda was in deep thought. "So, give me the Intel on this dude, what kind of numbers are we talking?" Luda asked.

"He's doing seven figures. He's a flashy clown that needs to be shown he's not untouchable," Mesha smiled as she sipped on the Ace of Spades.

"OOOOH shit. I knew what I meant to tell you. Me and Neeka came here together," Luda said. "Random thought, my bad."

"What she doing here?" Mesha asked

Luda licked his lips, rubbed his hands together, then said, "Her people are headed to the Outer Banks or some shit. Plus, she fucking with some nigga here," he answered.

"Bruh, why you all swole? Mad you sat on that too long?" Mesha joked.

Luda had time before now to approach Neeka, but never took advantage of the opportunity.

"Yo, you rolling with me later to her fam's cookout for the Fourth?" Luda asked.

"Yeah, because I haven't seen her fine ass brother Jamari in a minute," Mesha smiled. Luda sucked his teeth and then said, "Whatever!"

Meech kissed Neeka soon as he saw her. "Damn, bae, I guess you did miss me," Neeka smiled.

As he came up for air, he smiled. "Hell yeah. You didn't know?"

Luda watched the two, and it wasn't a friendly look when he passed by. Neeka waited until Luda was out of sight before she released her from her embrace. Luda had never stepped out of pocket the entire time they had known each other. It caught her totally off-guard. She couldn't deny that an attraction did exist, but she knew his lifestyle. While Luda was taking some night classes, there was an edge to him – way more than what met the eye. Meech was stability in her eyes. Someone who she could have a future with, and who was already filling her heart. She knew Meech had his flaws too, plus, he was going through a divorce, but he was the better of the two evils. He had shown her a different side that was loving, affectionate, and supporting. "I miss you too bae," she smiled as she put her face in the nape of his neck.

Meech was finally getting what Lucci had confessed about his love for Shanice because the things he lacked doing for Zeneka, he wanted to do for Neeka.

Neeka was confused on whether to tell Meech about the kiss, or about Luda altogether. She knew that he would be at the beach because her parents had invited him. She didn't want Meech to get blindsided in case Luda wanted to act like a nigga. Back in the day she was crushing on him, but those days was gone once she got wind of the fact he was a jack boy. She couldn't deny the physical attraction between them, but her heartbeat for Meech. She knew that Luda's trip was more business than personal.

***

Hours later, Meech was pulling up to a Colonial style house, dressed in brick, painted black. "Oh, honey this house is beautiful," Neeka wowed. She was excited to see the inside. The yard was so pretty with what looked like peonies and a crawling rose bush. The lawn itself looked like a vacuumed carpet.

"I told you, baby, I'm over that stupid shit. I hope you like it. Hopefully, you will be here living in it with me one day," Meech beamed.

She had told him that peonies and black-eyed Susan were her favorites, and he planted them in his flowerbed. Even though they were out of season due to the summer, she knew that in the spring, as broad as the base was, they would be beautiful. She couldn't wait to see what colors they would be. Tears welled up in Neeka's eyes because she had never imagined that she and Meech would get to this point so quickly.

Meech reached over to hug her and wipe her eyes, "I told you I'm serious. Cut the faucet off," he said chuckling. "Let's go let you see the inside."

Minutes later, Neeka's eyes were flooded with blues, dark

browns, and coral colors. His furniture was dark brown, and his drapes were blue with specks of brown that sat off the room's ambiance. "C'mon, let me give you the tour," Meech said taking her hand and giving her the grand tour of the home. After she had received the full tour, which she was truly impressed by, she collapsed on the couch.

"Baby, are you okay?" Meech asked concerned.

"Yeah, babe just jet-lagged. I need a nap," she smiled, but also in the back of her mind, she knew she needed to talk about the kiss from Luda. Right now, she was with the man she loved, so all was right with the world in her eyes.

"So, what's the schedule of events?" Meech asked. He pulled her feet to his lap, took her slides off, and began to rub her feet.

She was so tired, and that foot massage was on point. Closing her eyes, she said, "Well, my parents are flying in on Wednesday which gives us two days before we need to head to the coast. How far is the drive?"

Smiling from ear to ear Meech responded, "With my expert driving, about five hours."

"That's a ride, but I look forward to just being in your space. Plus, if we can't handle a road trip, this relationship is doomed."

"I know right. Do we need to help with groceries or anything? I'd be more than happy to contribute to the rental. I actually have a spot not too far where they are staying in Kitty Hawk. If you don't mind, I'd like to take you by there so you can see it."

"Wow – big money grip. That's your new name," Neeka said rubbing her thumb and fingers.

"What time do we need to be there on Friday?" Meech implored as Neeka drifted off. "Five o'clock babe," she mumbled. Meech picked her up and laid her in his bed.

"Come lay with me," Neeka cooed. Meech embraced her as they dozed off to sleep.

***

Zeneka was putting on the finishing touches of her make-up when Jamari called. She recognized his ring tone, "Candy Girl" by New Edition, and dove across the bed fumbling with the phone. Trying to calm her voice when she answered she said, "Hello, sunshine! I'm almost ready," Zeneka teased knowing Jamari was a stickler for time.

"Did you invite your friends for the Fourth? The more the merrier," Jamari assured her. Zeneka smiled because unlike Meech, he was cool with her circle.

"Yes, babe, they might be bringing plus ones," Zeneka responded.

"That's cool. Pops always overcook," he assured her. "You just need to let me know how many. I'm guessing six. The place sleeps fourteen, so we should be good on space."

"Okay, that sounds like a plan. We also have a place not too far away, so if need be, I can bunk there. Whatever is convenient. Give me ten minutes, and I will be ready," she assured Jamari.

Jamari picked her up like they had agreed on. Minutes later, they were looking for a place to park because the lot was packed. Zeneka and Jamari, over the last two months, had been spending a lot of time together. He was cool as hell. They really complimented each other well. He was well-traveled thanks to the United States Military. He had seen so many places and people and told the best stories. He made you want to fly to the United Arab Emirates just to see the beauty of it or to Venice to walk along the canals. Tonight, they were doing something she hadn't done in a minute, bowling.

He was a Chevy man and drove a Suburban. It was nice actually sitting up in a vehicle. She thought she saw a familiar face, Charday Funderburk. She and Charday went to high school together. Last Zeneka heard, she was engaged to Demetrius Barksdale. They had been high school sweethearts, and from what she understood via Facebook, they were engaged and to be married soon. That didn't look like Demetrius to Zeneka, but then again, none of that mattered, hell she had her own troubles.

Jamari walked over to her side of the car to open the door for Zeneka. He was so old school. He would always open the door to a building or a car. When they walked, he either held her hand or placed his hand on the small of her back. He touched her constantly. She went from little to no touching in a relationship, to constantly touching. It was a bit overwhelming.

Outside of the kiss he gave her on the cheek that night at Edith's, he had not tried to make a move on Zeneka. Jamari had managed to do something she had not done since before she was married, he courted her. He, quite frankly, was confusing her. When they first met, he was so aggressive. She thought that he would have her panties around her ankles and panting on the first date, and quite frankly she would've enjoyed it, but he had surprised her at every turn. She had actually gained a friend before she gained a lover, and regardless of how their relationship went, she would always be grateful to him for giving her broken heart time to mend.

Taking her hand and helping her step down from the truck, Jamari couldn't help but admire her simplicity. Her hair was up in a ponytail full of barrel curls, hanging just above her shoulders. Zeneka had on some distressed jeans and a chocolate t-shirt with an outline of an afro and a raised fist that said, "Don't Touch My Hair." She was poured into those jeans and had ass for days, plus, it was soft as drugstore cotton as his grandfather would say. He had held back for a minute because he didn't want to push her where she wasn't ready to go. Tonight, was different though. He just wanted to test the waters.

He pulled her close to him when she stepped out of the truck, left the door open, and pushed her back towards the seat. Holding her around her waist, he leaned down and placed his lips on hers chastely at first, but then used his tongue to gain entrance to her mouth. She moaned, and that literally pushed him over the edge. Moving his hands to her hips, he lifted her against his rock-hard erection and deepened the kiss.

Her nipples were so hard he could feel them against his

chest. Her hands went to the nape of his neck and twirled around the wisps of hair that had fallen out of his man bun. His hair was his Achilles heel. She had unknowingly unleashed the dragon.

Pop! Pop! Pop!

Shots rang out, and immediately Jamari went into protection mode. Pushing Zeneka into the car, he used the open door as a cover and made his way to the opposite side of the car.

"Lay down, Zeneka. I'm fine. Call 911 and let them know that shots have been fired." Awkwardly laying across the seats, Zeneka grabbed her cell from her pocket and did as she was told.

It was over as soon as it had begun. People began pouring out of the bowling alley to see what had happened. Sirens could be heard in the distance, so help was on the way. Making sure it was safe to move from his position, Jamari slowly crept out from behind the Suburban. He saw a face he hadn't seen in years holding his arm.

"What the fuck Gotti? No means no, man. I told you I was too pretty for you," Jamari said grabbing his old friend in a loose hug. "Did you see the shooter?"

"No, I was too preoccupied, but I have an idea," Gotti said surprised to see his old friend. In the Unit, they called him the "The Hitta," but according to the United States Marine Corp, he was Jamari, also known as one bad motherfucker. Not to brag, but they all were. Everyone "retired," and that is saying something based on the shit that they had to go through for the country they loved.

Gotti turned his attention to Charday and lifted her from her position on the ground. Jamari could see why Gotti was so pissed. She was a quiet storm of beauty and veritable brick house, not that he was looking, but damn. There was something about her that made you want to get on a horse and charge the next dumb ass that tried to come near her. It was how he felt about Zeneka and knew his friend well enough based on the look he had in his eyes to know that he was in deep.

Gotti was checking Charday over for injuries when the ambulance arrived. Jamari knew that he would decline assistance. Looked like a flesh wound. The bullet had skimmed across his arm. Luckily, no one was hurt. Jamari walked back over to the truck to check on Zeneka, but before he left, he gave Gotti his new number, and they agreed to meet up for coffee to catch up. Zeneka was surprised to see Charday with Gotti. "Hey, chick," Charday smiled.

"Hey, are y'all okay?" Zeneka asked.

Gotti looked at everyone then said, "I believe this is the work of my baby momma."

Gotti recognized Zeneka but didn't say anything because he heard that her and Meech, his close friend, were divorcing.

"Damn, you must have pissed her off," Jamari joked trying to bring light to the situation.

Charday was visibly shaken as Zeneka tried to console her.

"This is some bullshit. Her rejected ass doing the most," Charday yelped.

"I know, sis. The bitch killed our night," a pissed Zeneka sighed.

Jamari walked closer to check on Zeneka and noticed the dent in the side of the truck. His paranoia and the enemies he had created along the way, made Jamari bullet proof all the cars that he had. In this instance, he was glad that he did or either he or Zeneka would've been seriously wounded.

"Babe, I'm just glad that you're okay," Jamari chimed.

Zeneka sat in Jamari's truck pissed that their night was ruined. Jamari immediately pulled her out of the truck and stood her up to make sure she knew it would be plenty time for them. He hugged her tight, rubbed her back to soothe her, and told her that it was ok. Her tears made something come to the surface that hadn't in a long time – his anger. He'd be taking Gotti up on that coffee. No one fucked with what he claimed, even if it was an accident. Thirty-minutes later, they were at Alvin's. It was a secluded diner on the west side of Charlotte. All four filed into the diner. They walked in and found a table.

"So, long time, no see," Zeneka greeted Gotti. Jamari shot Gotti a bewildered look.

"So, y'all two know each other?" Jamari inquired.

Charday spoke up and responded, "Yes, Gotti is good friends with Meech."

Gotti quickly responded, "I pass no judgment on anyone.

As you can see, I have my own shit." Everyone laughed at his comments.

"Thanks for that Gotti," Zeneka chimed.

"Hell, I feel you. I was engaged to one of those Barksdale men also. They can be some assholes," Charday teased.

Gotti interjected, "Aight now, them my folks."

Jamari was listening to all of the comments when he pried, "Y'all talking like this family the mob."

Gotti quickly changed the conversation. "So, how long y'all been kicking it?"

Jamari picked up on how quickly Gotti changed the subject of the conversation. Everyone else followed suit.

"We're fresh and enjoying it," Jamari smiled as he rubbed Zeneka's hand.

"So, the Barksdale's, are they a family or an organization?" Jamari asked.

Zeneka patted his hand and said, "Honey, let it go. It's my past." Gotti and Charday were now buried in the menu.

"You right, I'm sorry for prying," Jamari apologized.

An hour later, everyone had ordered, eaten, and renewed friendships. "Well, I have church in the morning," Zeneka said.

"Well, bruh it was good catching up," Jamari added. Minutes later, they were parting ways.

"We definitely have to do this again," Charday said.

"Girl, you know my number," Zeneka responded.

Minutes later as Zeneka and Jamari were driving away, she consoled Jamari, "My past nor my ex is a threat to you."

Jamari retorted, "I was out of line. My curiosity got the best of me. It just puzzled me when everyone shutdown at my question, but that's no excuse."

Feeling obligated to answer, she answered short and sweet, "I will tell you this: The Barksdale family is very powerful and generous to those they love, but faithfulness to the one they love isn't their strong suit."

"Honey, no explanation needed," Jamari confirmed.

"I know, but I felt I needed to assure you, so you wouldn't have to wonder," Zeneka offered as Jamari pulled in front of her house. "Well, the evening has been eventful," Zeneka smiled as she gathered her purse.

"Yeah, it has been," Jamari co-signed and turned off the truck. "Let me walk you to the door," Jamari said as he unfastened his seatbelt.

"I see there are still some gentlemen left in the world," Zeneka welcomed.

"Yeah, it's a part of courting," Jamari answered sarcastically.

"Thank you for understanding me not wanting to be physical right away," Zeneka cooed.

"No problem, you're worth the wait," he assured her.

Zeneka pulled out her keys and walked in her house, then she turned on her heel and said, "Goodnight."

Again, Jamari was disappointed, but she still piqued his interest. Minutes later, he was driving away.

Chapter Fourteen
THE SET-UP

Mesha and Luda had staked out Lucci's house for hours. "Sis, where this nigga at?" Luda had told Mesha to park on the opposite side of the road, so he could make a clean getaway.

"Duck, that's his car coming!" Mesha shrieked.

She and Luda ducked down as Lucci passed them heading home. Luda cocked his gun, hit the safety as he opened the door, and started the trek to Lucci's house. Luda hid in the shadows waiting on Lucci to get to the door, the neighborhood the houses were within an earshot of each other, and he knew in a subdivision there was always traffic and nosey neighbors. Minutes later, Lucci got out of his Lexus GSL coupe and grabbed two duffel bags. Lucci walked up his walkway without noticing Luda. Just as he got to his door Luda ran up behind him. Lucci felt the 9mm press against the middle of his back. "You know what this is. Open the fucking door," Luda scuffed.

"This not what you want, partner," Lucci laughed. Not believing someone would be this bold to hit him up, so he was hesitant at first. Just as he opened the door, he felt the butt of the gun come crashing down on the back of his head. He fell to the floor as blood squirted out and soaked the back of his shirt.

As Lucci tried to get his bearings, Luda rummaged through the two duffel bags. One was full of weed, and the other was full of bands of money. *Jackpot,* Luda said to himself as he drug the duffel bags outside.

Lucci was still reeling from the blow. When he regained his composure he said, "Whoever you are, you just signed your death certificate." His vision was blurry, and all he saw was a figure dressed in all black. Luda knew he had to hurry up. Just as Lucci tried to get up, he came down with another blow with the 9mm onto his forehead. Blood gushed from Lucci's head and splattered everywhere. "Agghh, motherfucker you better kill me," Lucci yelled as he began to lose consciousness. As he fell to the floor, Luda let off two slugs that ripped through Lucci's upper body and knee, knocking him to the floor.

"Your wish is my command, motherfucker," Luda laughed. Luda grabbed the bags and closed the door behind him as he left Lucci to die. As Luda crossed the street, he looked back and figured the neighbors heard the gunshots because he saw a lady in her robe on the phone. "Aight, let's get the hell outta here," Luda yelled to Mesha. Mesha saw the blood on Luda's black joggers, and she knew that he had wreaked havoc.

"Slow down, your nervous ass," Luda teased as he fired up a blunt.

"Nigga, a bitch is nervous," Mesha responded as the police sped past them.

"Was the lick worth it?" Mesha said as she greedily eyed the duffel bags.

"I will know once I get back to your spot," Luda grinned.

Mesha was having second thoughts about the set-up now. She could tell by the blood splattered on Luda's clothes that Lucci didn't fare well. Plus, she had since learned that the Barksdale family ran the city. Her biggest worry was getting out of town because she knew that with those type of connects, it wouldn't be long before karma was darkening her doorstep.

"Good look-out sis. These types of licks will keep a nigga like me around this town," Luda teased. Mesha was fidgety as she pulled into her apartment complex parking lot. Luda saw that she was noticeably shaking and said, "Hit this blunt, or take a drink when we get inside to calm your ass down."

They exited the car. Mesha was still slightly paranoid as they disappeared into her apartment.

Lucci thought to himself as he lay on the ground losing consciousness, "I can't believe this motherfucker just shot me." Time seemed as if it was going in slow motion as he felt himself fighting to stay conscious. The bullets burned his flesh. He was in excruciating pain. He could hear people talking to him trying to see what was happening.

He could hear sirens blaring as he tried in vain to remove the bulletproof vest. His neighbor was calling his name. As the sirens got closer, people filed toward his house to see what was going on. Fifteen minutes later, "Sir, can you tell us your name?" the blonde medic asked. Lucci floated in and out of consciousness as she pried the bulletproof vest and blood-soaked shirt off.

Shanice pushed her way through the crowd. She was blocked by a police officer, "Ma'am, please step back." Shanice could see through the doorway even though she was denied entry. She saw the blood splattered, and the EMT hovered over him. Tears ran down her face as she saw them place him on the gurney. The officer at the door yelled, "Clear the way!"

Shanice was going to surprise him and tell him she was pregnant. When the gurney rolled into view, Lucci looked lifeless on the gurney blanket. "OMG, Lucci," she screamed as they hurried past her. She was balling her eyes out.

"Are you okay ma'am?" the cop asked, seeing how emotional she was.

"That's my baby's father," she said as she leaned into his chest crying.

"I'm so sorry," the cop said trying to console her.
****

Luda was feeling himself as he counted out the money. Mesha's mind worked overtime with regret because she knew that her scheming had signed her and Luda's death certificate.

Noticing how fidgety she was, Luda said to her, "I can literally see you overthinking."

Mesha flashed a fake smile then lied, "Naw, I'm good. Just feeling the effects of that exotic."

She knew their biggest worry wasn't the police, but more so the Barksdales. She was so bent on revenge that she didn't think everything out, but knew it was too late for it now.

"One-hundred, twenty-thousand dollars in cash, about forty-thousand drugs," Luda exclaimed as he slid twenty thousand towards Mesha.

She eyed the money, not really wanting it, but she knew the money was needed because she had thought out an escape plan for herself. "Bruh, don't get caught up in this town. I'm out," Mesha chimed.

Luda smiled at her comments then responded," Thanks for the advice, but I'm going to be here for a while."

Mesha sighed at his response then quickly said, "You're welcomed to stay here, but I'm on the next thing smoking."

"I see your ass still scary as hell," Luda laughed. Mesha rose up, headed to her room to pack.

Chapter Fifteen
NEW DIRECTIONS

Hours Later...

Meech was half unconscious lying across the bed. Neeka was watching television reruns of Martin. His phone started ringing uncontrollably, he sat up and grabbed his phone. Neeka eyeballed him as he answered to Shanice balling on the phone.

"Meech, someone shot him," she wailed inaudibly.

Neeka could tell by his facial expression it wasn't good. "Who? What the fuck?"

"I'm on my way to the hospital. It didn't look good," she blubbered.

"Calm down for a second. Where are they taking him?" Meech yelled.

"CMC main. I'll be in the waiting room," she sniffled.

"Okay, I'm on my way," Meech said frantically as he ended

the call. Meech grabbed his keys and grabbed Neeka's hand, "Babe, c'mon. My brother has been shot."

"Okay, babe let me grab my shoes," Neeka answered.

Meech was pacing back and forth. Thirty-minutes later, Meech walked into the waiting room and was met by Shanice.

"Wassup, what are they saying?" Meech grimaced.

"They just wheeled him back, so it's a waiting game," she answered. Shanice's eyes were noticeably puffy.

Neeka scanned the waiting room when she blurted out, "Jamari, what are you doing here?"

He was so enthralled in conversation with Zeneka that Neeka caught him and Zeneka off-guard. Jamari nearly leaped from his chair.

"I didn't know you had arrived," he smiled as he gave her a bear hug.

Already on edge, Meech snapped, "Who is this, and why is he all hugged up on you?"

He also noticed that the stranger he was asking about had come from the direction where he had seen Zeneka sitting. Zeneka looked his way, rolled her eyes, and looked away.

"I'm sorry, baby, this my brother," Neeka said as they released their embrace.

"How you doing? I'm Jamari," Jamari greeted.

Neeka spoke up as Meech was hesitant to speak, "Who are you with?"

"I'm sorry, bruh, I'm Meech. I'm dating your sister," Meech smiled.

Jamari responded dryly realizing that he was Zeneka's

soon to be ex-husband, "Nice to meet you. I'm here with my girl Zeneka. Her brother-in-law got shot. Hey, babe come meet my sister," Jamari smiled.

Zeneka walked over to them, and Neeka noticed Shanice and Meech's demeanor change.

Jamari gushed as he said, "This my girl, Zeneka, sis. This, this is my sister, Neeka."

"Nice to meet you," Zeneka smiled as she grabbed Jamari's hand to piss Meech off.

"Yeah, your brother is something special," Zeneka cooed, pouring it on to be petty.

Interrupting the conversation Meech spat, "Baby, this is my soon to be ex-wife, Zeneka."

Jamari and Neeka both looked at each other with a confused look. Shanice saw the situation was about to get messy and redirected the conversation by saying, "Meech, can you see if they have any new updates?"

Meech just responded, "Yeah, I need some fresh air."

Jamari's suspicions were confirmed as he gave Zeneka a disapproving look.

"Hold on, babe, I will go with you," Neeka sneered as she rolled her eyes at Zeneka and walked away with Meech.

Zeneka and Jamari headed to a secluded corner. Shanice was being consoled by her parents. Minutes later, Absalom and Vincent walked into the room. Everyone's eyes beamed on them as they scanned the room. Minutes later, Meech returned and saw them looking for a seat, "Wassup, Unk?"

"Nothing, heard about what happened," a concerned Absalom said.

Not realizing who his dad was at first he said, "Wassup, Vincent. How are you?"

The scowl on his face showed that his words burned Vincent, but he let it slide.

"So, what's his status?" Vincent asked.

"He just left surgery, and now he's waiting on a room," the doctor announced to everyone.

"The Barksdale family," a nurse yelled into the waiting room.

Everyone paraded towards the door into the hallway where they met with the surgeon. The surgeon, a gray-haired, white gentleman said, "Well, we made it through surgery. He flat-lined once, but we got him back."

Shanice gasped and felt weak at the doctor's words. Zeneka and Meech rushed over to her side. "Are you aight?" Meech questioned. Shanice shook her head yes, and Meech fell back.

Zeneka was at her side. "Are you really okay?" Zeneka whispered.

"Yeah, girl," Shanice lied.

Absalom pulled Meech to the side and asked, "Wassup with Shanice? Why is she taking it so hard?"

Not one to reveal Lucci's business he said, "I don't know Unk."

"Well, we have him sedated. Time will tell," the doctor ended.

"Well, whatever he needs, no matter the price, you give it to him," Vincent spat.

The doctor just shook his hand and answered, "Yes, sir." As he shook Vincent's hand, everyone was in awe of his declaration.

"Please, everyone keep Lucci in your prayers," Absalom commanded as everyone dispersed. He had put two and two together but wanted confirmation. Absalom signaled Shanice over.

"So, you mixing business with pleasure, Shanice?" Absalom inquired.

A surprised Shanice deflected his question by saying, "Are we still on for our meeting Wednesday?"

Absalom picked up on her move then answered, "Touché', baby girl." Shanice had always respected what the elder Barksdale men thought of her seeing that they had a lot to do with her career upswing, but regardless of who it was, she wasn't going to hide her love for Lucci. In her mind, Lucci was her future. The growth she saw in him convinced her that he was meant to be her husband.

A few days later...

Absalom, Vincent, Damien, and Anthony were all sitting in Shanice's boardroom. "Hello everyone," Shanice greeted them as she sat a folder in front of each of them.

Everyone responded. Anthony's head dropped after looking at the contents of the folder. "How bad has he fucked up now?" Vincent quizzed as he looked at Anthony with disappointment.

"It's pretty serious because women were brought across interstate lines," Shanice answered.

"So how can we make this go away?" Absalom inquired, tapping his finger on the table with aggravation.

"What the fuck was you thinking?" Damien said as he slammed his fist on the table.

"Pops, I didn't. She was underage," Anthony defended to his father and cousin Damien.

"Alright, I'm going to need y'all to calm down," Shanice snapped.

"Is it too late to keep a lid on this?" Vincent asked as he rubbed his beard with a frustrated look.

"I already have that covered as best as we can," Shanice smiled confidently. Feeling herself getting sick Shanice lied, "I have another meeting, but I'm on top of it."

All the men rose from the table to exit the boardroom. Minutes after, they left, and she rushed to her personal restroom to empty her guts. Shanice was wrenching, doubled over the toilet when her secretary rushed in.

"Are you okay, Shanice?" she asked.

Shanice shook her head that she was fine. Her secretary handed her a tissue.

In between wrenching, Shanice said, "I believe it's a twenty-four-hour virus."

"It's a lot of that going around," her secretary agreed. "Well, if you need me, I'm at my desk."

Shanice regained her composure and made it to her desk to pack up her briefcase.

Chapter Sixteen
USED AND ABUSED

Next Day

Zania was sipping on a glass of wine as she was sprawled out on the couch thinking how she was going to tell Zeneka about Meech being Javon's father, but she figured if she convinced Rozay to fight for her love, it would keep her distracted and Meech would be hers. In her mind, Javon was where he belonged, with her. As she poured another glass of Chablis, there was a knock at the door. She was hesitant to open the door, so she peeped out of her blinds and saw it was Shanice.

"Awww *shit*," she muttered to herself. She rolled her eyes and sucked her teeth, "What the hell she want?" She looked confused when she yanked the door open, "What's wrong with you?"

Her words opened the floodgates as Shanice walked into the house. "Somebody shot my baby," she cried.

"What? Who? Huh?" a confused and tipsy Zania asked.

"I went to tell Meech about me being pregnant, but when I arrived, it was a crime scene. I later learned that he had been shot," she whined.

Zania was shocked as she tried to have compassion for Shanice and Lucci As emotionally detached as Zania was, Shanice was her friend, and she was going to be there for her. She hugged Shanice as they made their way to the couch to sit.

"Are you okay? Do you want something to eat or drink?" Zania offered as she resumed sipping her Chablis.

Shanice then blurted out, "OMG, Zania what am I going to do?" she whined as tears soaked her face. "I don't want to do this alone."

"Calm down, catch your breath," Zania coached.

Shanice was visibly shaken as she closed her eyes. She laid her head back to get her thoughts together as tears streamed down her eyes.

"So, it's finally confirmed that you're pregnant?" Zania pried. Never one with tact or filter she blurted out, "Well, at least our kids will be cousins."

Anger ran through Shanice's body.

"Bitch, do you hear your fucking self-right now?" Shanice snapped as she sat up on the couch. "Why are you so fucking heartless? That's your sister's husband."

Zania knew her comment was fucked up, so she tried to

play it off as a joke. She rolled her eyes, flipped her hair, and said, "I was joking. Calm your pregnant ass down," Zania joked.

"Let me get out of here. It's getting late," Shanice sighed grabbing her purse.

"Girl, stop tripping and sit down," Zania frowned.

"Naw, I'm good," Shanice said and stood up as Zania sipped her wine. Just as she opened the door, she almost bumped into Rozay coming in. "Ohhh shit, you scared me, Rozay," she said as he stepped to the side.

"Zania, you got company," Shanice spat, who didn't speak as she walked by.

Rozay was surprised at her flippant attitude and the fact she didn't speak.

"What's wrong with her?" Rozay asked, who was met only by Zania's cold stare.

"What you doing just popping up at my house?" Zania hissed. Her words fell on deaf ears as he walked in uninvited. "Seriously, you know my number. Don't be popping up. That's some stalker shit. So, after tonight, stop." Rozay frowned at her comment.

"I think we need to talk," Rozay smiled as he sat down next to a tipsy Zania.

"Now, tell me exactly why it is so urgent for us to talk," she hissed.

"I know you're fucking your sister's husband," he teased.

Zania frowned at his statement. "I know your black ass not trying to blackmail me," Zania snapped.

Rozay threw his hands up in defense then reiterated, "No, baby, you got it all wrong. I was just saying you want him, I want her, but this new motherfucker cock blocking. His ass has got to go."

"So how you assume we accomplish this?" Zania sighed.

"You pump me up to your sister and run interference between Meech and his new chick."

"Now, why would I want to do that?" she smiled as she poured another glass of wine.

"So, you not going to offer me any of that wine?" Rozay flirted.

"This your second time popping up at my shit. Hell, you need to be asking what bill is due," she fussed.

"What brings you to these parts?" she said jokingly.

"I wanted to see how my favorite side chick was doing," he sneered.

Zania had been around Rozay enough to know when something was going on with him. Seeing he was on some bullshit she asked, "Do you smoke?" Rozay shook his head yes. "You want me to roll us a blunt?" Zania asked.

"That's cool. I need something to relax me," Rozay answered as he sat down on the sofa. "I guess you can take the girl out of the ghetto, but not the ghetto out of the girl," he added.

"Fuck you," Zania fumed. The aroma of marijuana filled the living room as Zania pulled on the blunt.

"Those lips are good at wetting things up," Rozay giggled as the contact from the weed changed his mood.

Zania smiled and responded, "You right, the Barksdale's got me this two-hundred, forty-thousand-dollar house." "Hell, I popped up on your sister ass too. She was pissed about it," he laughed "Because you be on some stalker shit," snapped Zania

Rozay's facial expression turned to a grimace, "Smart ass! Pass me that blunt."

The weed and Chablis had Zania lit as she rose from the sofa. Zania was now standing up dancing, twerking her hips as Young Thug played in the background. Rozay's eyes danced in his head as her hips ground from side to side.

"Damn, that ass looking good," he said as he inhaled the smoke from the blunt. "This Kush is straight fire. Got a nicca on instant tilt."

Zania looked over her shoulder as she now purposely made her ass jiggle as she danced. Rozay felt his dick rising as the effects of the marijuana started to take over.

Zania was now bending down as her ass danced in her leggings that clung to her ass. She noticed the rising in Rozay's jeans.

"Damn, boo. What you got going on in those jeans?" she teased while twerking her ass slowly.

Rozay smiled at her comments as his dick rose even more. "This tower needs a climber," he giggled.

Zania was truly blitzed from the effects of the weed. Her pussy throbbed and looking at his hard dick in his jeans didn't help any. "Come over here, let me knock that tower down," she commanded as she started to take her clothes off.

Rozay stood up, and his jeans fell to his ankles. His dick was standing tall in his boxers. As he pulled them down, Zania's eyes lit up like headlights. His dick gave a thud when he finally released it. She was now in front of him on her knees massaging it as the pre-cum seeped with excitement.

Her hand gripped his cock and her saliva coated the head as she engulfed it, slowly coating it as she massaged it with her tongue. Saliva dripped from the tip to his balls.

"You like that, don't you?" she murmured as she slowly massaged his balls. She sucked his dick like a kid eating an ice cream cone on a hot day. After minutes of him feeling her up and her stroking him off, Zania was hot and ready.

"Damn baby I need that in me," she murmured.

Rozay rose up and took control. "You know I'm about to taste this pussy, right?" he stammered. Zania fell back on the couch and pinned her legs back so her pussy was fully exposed to him. He dove in headfirst. His tongue slid up and down the folds of her pussy lips, which were swollen, as he gently sucked on the clit. His tongue snaked around it as she let out a sigh of pleasure. She lightly bit down on her lip as he worked his tongue.

"Motherfucker, that shit feel so good," she moaned as his tongue worked her clit like a stripper working a pole.

Her hips met his every lick. Her pussy soaked the couch like a running faucet. Her hips bucked like a stallion, and her hands gripped his head as she came. "You're a nasty motherfucker," she yelped as the words slurred from the intensity of her body convulsing. Her pussy squirted her juices everywhere. Zania and Rozay had moved to the bedroom where she was face down, ass in the air, as he rhythmically moved in and out of her pussy.

"Long, deep strokes," Zania moaned as his dick explored parts of her pussy no one had before.

Her wet pussy engulfed his long dick. Pussy juices trickled on the bed. The more she moaned, the deeper he dug.

"Who's beating this pussy up?" Rozay chimed. He gave her his full length and let it rest at the bottom of her pussy. Her hips ground while he did so. She ground on his dick like she was dancing on a pole.

"Push that motherfucker deep in that pussy. I want to feel it in my stomach," she moaned.

"Flip your ass on your back!" he commanded.

Zania was on her back on the edge of the bed as Rozay towered over her. He had her legs pinned back as he looked at his long, ebony cock disappear in and out of her juicy, wet pussy which was soaking the comforter on the bed.

"Oh, shit. I can feel that black snake hitting my ovaries," Zania said as Rozay smiled at the joy he was giving her.

His strokes sped up going deeper and faster as her pussy contracted around his dick with every stroke. "Oh shit," he moaned as his dick erupted. He pumped harder.

"Damn, this pussy won't stop cumming!" Zania yelled as he collapsed on top of her. Rozay knew he was foul for fucking Zania, but he didn't give a fuck because he figured that Zania was doing her thing.

"Aight, so you gonna help me land your sister?" a buzzed Rozay joked.

Zania frowned at his words. "Didn't you just fuck me? What the fuck was in that weed? Nigga, you foul and flagrant."

"Do she know you fucking her husband?" Rozay joked.

"So, if I say no, then what? You rat me out to my sister?" Zania asked. "I thought only petty bitches did that."

Disappointed by her response, he grew agitated. "Naw I'm not, are you going to help me?" an anxious Rozay questioned.

"I'll pass because my name's on Meech's dick forever," Zania giggled.

As her words struck his ears, he let them soak in, and then something in him snapped. Rozay's eyes became dark quick. Zania, tipsy or not, picked up on his demeanor change. She knew she needed to go with the flow. Rozay jumped up and walked over to Zania, then he threatened, "Listen here, you two- dollar, fuck-anything-moving, bitch. If you don't rock with me, you will regret it."

"Can you please step the fuck back?" Zania fumed as she felt threatened in her space. "I'm not your trick or your bitch, now step the fuck back. You might want to Google my crazy ass," she yelled.

Rozay reached down and grabbed her hair, wrapping it around his hand.

"Like I said, you little bitch, I'm your daddy now," he growled.

She was swinging, but her punches only landed body blows.

"Let my hair go, motherfucker," Zania fumed, trying to pry her hair loose. "Okay, okay. I will do it. Let my fucking hair go," she whined.

"That's a girl," he growled as he released her hair.

She looked at him and rolled her eyes. Rozay smiled as he grabbed her drink and finished it off.

"Ok, I hear you. Now, get the fuck out of my house. It's late," Zania hissed.

Rozay smiled, turned on his heel to leave, then said, "I will be in touch, and this better stay between us."

She wanted her truths to be revealed at her own discretion. She now knew what it felt like to now be the victim. She knew that he could make her life miserable. She wanted to be the one who told Zania.

***

The day seemed pointless for the two detectives, Hamilton and Ferguson. No matter where they turned, a dead-end. They had no luck finding whoever was bold enough to pull off such a hit. They had come to the conclusion that they would have to go directly to Lucci to see who had shot him and left him for dead. They knew Lucci lived by the code of the street and was probably not going to talk. They knew they would have a better chance of getting ice water in hell. Lucci would never give them any information about what went down with his shooting. They finally made it to the hospital, parked the squad car, and exited. They made their way up the long walkway leading to the entrance. The detectives entered the hospital and made their way to the front desk.

"How may I help you officers?" the desk clerk asked.

"We need to find out the status of someone," Ferguson inquired.

"Who is the patient?" she asked nervously.

"Lucci Barksdale," Hamilton huffed. "He was in ICU. We were wondering if he had been placed in a room."

"Hold on one second, I can check the records for you," the nurse answered. Ferguson checked out the surroundings of the hospital and how many renovations had been done to the hospital since he was there last. "Mr. Barksdale is being placed in a room as we speak," she responded.

"It will be a while before we can talk with him. So, we might as well comb the streets," Ferguson said to Hamilton.

"Thank you," Hamilton politely gestured to the front desk attendant.

Hamilton and Ferguson knew they had to keep the shooting confidential, or they would have a mess on their hands. They knew the streets were about to get bloody once word reached Barksdale's crew.

***

Subconsciously, Lucci's mind played vivid memories of past events in his life. He knew he was in grave health because he could hear the doctors and nurses talk around him.

"He's a lucky man," he heard one doctor say. "If the gunshot would've been a little more to the right, even with the vest on, he wouldn't be alive today."

Lucci was grateful to be alive. The one thought that haunted his mind was why anyone would shoot him. He couldn't think of a time where he had shit on anyone in any of his dealings. Their creed had always been if I eat, you eat. His body ached all over. He was feeling the aftermath of the bullet that had invaded his body. He heard the monitor beep as doctors and nurses talked about his prognosis as though he were not there. It was like he had seen on television several times before. Although he was alert, he was in a deep sleep he couldn't awake from. The beeping monitors always reminded him that he had God's grace. His body ached at every move he made. He couldn't get the thought of someone targeting him out of his mind.

"Motherfucker," he thought to himself. Why would someone flex on his family? They had to know that hit would give them a one-way ticket to hell. Shanice, Vincent, and Meech had sat with him whenever their schedules allowed. He was grateful for the company, but most of the time she came he was so doped up on pain meds that he couldn't talk. It hurt him to see her in so much pain over him, but he was going to give her the commitment she wanted for riding from him.

Chapter Seventeen

KARMA'S AT YOUR DOOR

Meech was sitting in his office when his uncle, Absalom, walked in.

"Wassup, when did you get back from South Africa?" Meech asked as he gave him a firm handshake.

"About an hour ago," Absalom said as he collapsed on the couch. "How is my nephew recuperating?" a concerned Absalom asked.

"He's on the right track. Not quite one hundred yet," Meech explained.

"I'm glad to hear that. So, what's up with lining up a carrier for our shipments from overseas?" Absalom asked. "We always need a carrier for the Taiwan shipment going to Russia."

Meech scribbled all of Absalom orders down on his notepad.

"Okay, I will take care of it," Meech sighed.

Meech looked visibly stressed.

"You look tired or worried about something else. What's going on?" Absalom asked as he reclined on Meech's office sofa.

Meech dropped his head and sighed, "You know me and Zeneka divorcing, just reflecting," he answered.

Absalom shook his head, "I'm going to keep it serious with you. She was too good for you. You dogged her out chasing after them thot ass girls. What did you expect her to do?"

Meech got choked up at his uncle's response to him playing the victim.

"I agree. I did some foul shit. It fucked me up seeing her on the next man arm."

Absalom rubbed salt in the wound by saying, "Boy, she was looking too good at the hospital, wasn't she?"

Meech sighed, then tried to redirect the conversation.

"I also need you to cut Ferguson and Hamilton a check. We don't need the extra heat from CMPD as far as Lucci goes."

"I will put Vincent on it. That's his forte," Meech agreed. "So, when do you leave back out?"

Absalom stood up then answered, "Friday, I go to Jamaica to set up some shipments."

"Oh okay," Meech mumbled.

Seeing that he had made his point with Meech, Absalom knew he had to get with Vincent on some family matters, so he rose from the couch to leave. "Well, nephew just take it as a life lesson. Take care of those shipments. I'm outta here," Absalom consoled as he exited the office.

"Safe travels," Meech added.

"You will be traveling more too, I heard," Absalom said.

Meech reared back in his chair and sighed, "Yeah," as Absalom walked out of his office.

***

Vincent was sitting in his office puffing on a cigar when Hamilton and Ferguson walked in. He stood to greet both men. "What's going on fellas?" Vincent chimed.

"Nothing much. How are you, Vincent? It's been awhile," Ferguson concurred as they both sat down.

"Would you guys like something to drink?" Vincent offered. They both declined, wanting to get down to the matter at hand.

"Vincent, we went by the hospital to talk to Lucci, but we ran into a wall of excuses," Hamilton said slyly.

Vincent just smiled knowing that he had greased lot of palms to keep them out. He responded, "Really? We haven't had any problems."

Ferguson spoke up and said, "That wouldn't be due to your family's behalf, would it?"

"You sure I can't get you fellas anything to drink?" Vincent smiled as he grabbed a water from his cooler.

Hamilton took in the office that looked like a top-grade mancave. It was equipped with a fully stocked bar and a mounted projector screen. It looked more like a clubhouse.

The floors were covered with rustic, marble tile. Carolina Panthers memorabilia littered the walls.

"So, enough bullshitting fellas. How much to make this go away?" Vincent inquired cockily.

Ferguson rubbed his chin as Hamilton dropped his head. "You know offering us a bribe is a crime, right? Unless the number is on point," Hamilton joked. All of them burst out in laughter.

"I knew it was a reason I always liked you guys," Vincent smirked as he stood up from his desk, shifting stares from one to another.

"So, throw me a number fellas," Vincent said.

Hamilton scratched his head, then spoke up, "One hundred thousand." Ferguson smiled at the number. Vincent didn't flinch as he went into the bottom drawer of his desk. After a few minutes of him pulling out stacks of money, they were sitting on his desk when he was done. Both of the men greedily eyed the money. "Aight, fellas dig in," he said and let out a hearty laugh.

The detectives divided the money amongst themselves. "So, I take it this situation dead?" Vincent chimed.

Ferguson gave a blank stare, then grinned, "What situation?"

Vincent knew they would bite from previous dealings with them. "Thank you for your donation to our retirement funds," Hamilton joked.

"Glad to be able to help," Vincent agreed.

"You sure you fellas wouldn't care for a drink?" Vincent inquired.

"No but thank you. We need to be getting on," Ferguson answered as they stashed the cash on their person.

Vincent extended his hand to both detectives then sneered, "I do need a name for whoever shot my son. It will be greatly appreciated."

"Of course, you will be our first call," Hamilton responded as they walked out of the office.

"Vincent, we will be seeing you soon," Ferguson remarked.

Vincent smiled to himself and reclined back in his chair.

***

Thirty minutes later, on the other side of town......

"What in God's name is going on here?" Ferguson asked as he jumped out of the car with his gun drawn. The crowd stood around a man who had been shot in the leg and writhing in pain.

"Clear the way, let us through," Hamilton commanded.

Hamilton knelt down to see what was wrong with the victim who was half conscious and squirmed in pain. Ferguson kept the crowd at bay while Hamilton focused on the shooting victim. "Back the fuck up," Ferguson commanded as the crowd started to grow. The ambulance, followed by two police cruisers with their sirens blaring, roared down the street, catching the crowd's attention. The crowd now parted like the Red Sea as the medics rushed through the crowd.

The backup officers quickly corralled the crowd.

As Ferguson scanned the crowd, he noticed a woman

behind the crowd. It was someone familiar to him. It was Sadie, a neighborhood crackhead, whore, and scammer, but her only credibility was that she was always truthful. In the hood, that was rare.

Ferguson locked eyes with her, "Sadie, what happened here? Come talk to me."

Sadie, walked away, not to draw attention from the crowd. Ferguson ensued down the alleyway to talk unnoticed.

"Give me the story, Sadie. What went down here," he asked.

Sadie, still shook from the Italians, hesitated to talk. "It was Luda from what I heard," Sadie squealed.

Ferguson pressed on with the questioning. Sadie's uneasiness eventually became more prevalent as Ferguson's impatience was beginning to show. He got in her face.

"Alright, Sadie, I know you have information where I can find him," Ferguson demanded.

"Earlier, a gang of dudes came through looking for information about a robbery. We sell ass and gamble. We didn't know anything, so it turned ugly really quick," she responded.

"They raided the house looking for information. It was that heavy."

Ferguson listened attentively as she spilled off information like a faucet leaking water.

"Did you know any of the guys?" Ferguson asked.

"None of them looked familiar," Sadie said as she kept looking around to make sure no one saw them talking.

"Well, here, take my card. If you come across any more

information, call me," Ferguson said as Sadie walked toward the back exit of the alley. As Ferguson made it back to where the crowd had thinned out, the victim was now on a gurney getting loaded in the ambulance. He waved to Hamilton to come to him.

"Wassup, Ferguson?" Hamilton asked. "What you got because the victim was too scared to talk?"

"Well, my informant told me it was a bunch of unknowns," Ferguson answered.

"It has Barksdale's name written all over it," Hamilton said. "Well, we gonna sit back and let this unfold on its own."

Ferguson lit a cigarette and took a long draw. Hamilton's face grimaced as he exhaled the smoke, waving it away as the wind pushed it his way.

"You and those fucking cigarettes," Hamilton coughed.

"Boom, Boom!" exploded in the background as the two of them talked.

"What the fuck was that?" Ferguson asked. Both of them had drawn their guns.

"It came from that way, behind the house," Hamilton said as he raced to the back of the house. He found Sadie lying on the ground with a gunshot to her arm, gasping for air. Ferguson knelt down to ask her what happened as she writhed in pain.

"Sadie, did you see the shooter?" Ferguson asked.

"Hey, partner. We need to find who's doing this quickly," Hamilton sighed.

Sadie knew this was retribution from her having loose lips. So, she was now pleading the fifth.

***

After weeks of him begging, Zeneka agreed to meet Rozay, but in a public setting. She was secure in her life. The only thing that was unresolved was her slip-up with Rozay. She felt he was delusional to have any expectations afterward. He knew she was vulnerable. She was expecting a friendship, not a relationship.

Zeneka was dressed casual wearing a multi-colored sundress with a pair of peep-toe wedges. Her hair was in an isometric bob, and her jewelry matched her dress with accents. She was taking in the crowded college courtyard when she saw Rozay crossing it. He was dressed in Duck Headgear with some casual Sebago's. Zeneka sighed as he got closer. It was a breezy day, so the wind carried the scent of his D&G white cologne that intoxicated her nose.

"I see you're enjoying this beautiful weather," Rozay said as he removed his shades.

"Yeah, it's a beautiful day," Zeneka responded.

"Enough with the fake salutations, wassup?" Rozay pressed. Zeneka was taken aback by his anxiousness.

"See this is why I can't do you," Zeneka muttered as she waved him off.

"What did I do?" Rozay asked intrusively as he tapped his feet.

"I need you to respect my space," she moaned.

Getting aggravated, Rozay knew the courtyard was crowded, so he was careful of his tone.

"I haven't been getting at you, just a friendly text," Rozay huffed. Zeneka was watching his body language as she slid around more to face him.

"I see you sliding back. What you think I'm going to spazz out?" Rozay teased. Just as he was getting hype, Meech walked up.

Zeneka was actually glad to see him. Rozay was caught off-guard by his presence, as well as his body language.

"I guess you thought I was playing, Zeneka," Meech growled as he rolled up on them. "Dude, why are you entertaining my wife?" Meech grimaced.

Rozay was nonchalant to his aggressiveness.

"Why are you entertaining her sister?" Rozay shot back.

"Motherfucker, so you trying to cause chaos," Meech snapped as he moved closer to Rozay. Rozay jumped up to show Meech he wasn't intimidated.

"You mad because someone else finds your wife to be beautiful," Rozay scoffed.

"Y'all, please don't do this," Zeneka pleaded.

"I told you I wasn't playing this shit," Meech yelled.

"Why the fuck you tripping, dawg? Y'all not together," Rozay interjected as he pushed Meech in his chest.

"Don't fucking touch me, motherfucker," Meech snapped. Zeneka was frozen with fear, shocked at Meech's behavior.

Meech landed a punishing blow to Rozay's eye. Fear engulfed Zeneka. She had never seen this side of Meech. He followed up with an uppercut. Rozay blocked a barrage of punches that Meech threw but a majority of them landed.

"You're out doing shit. Is she not entitled to be able to move on as well?" Rozay questioned as he saw Zeneka was at a loss for words.

Zeneka screeched, "Please no, Meech, you don't need them troubles." Rozay was on the ground folded up and bruised.

"Man, we just friends. What the fuck?" Rozay scoffed as his eye had instantly swelled.

"You thought I wasn't going to get into your ass for fucking my wife?" Meech scowled as Rozay laid on the ground holding his hands up defensively.

"Dude, all the shit you've done. Really?" Rozay cowered.

"Meech, stop, please. He's not worth it," Zeneka pleaded, now standing between them.

Rozay, still shook, stood up battered and bruised, and spat, "So, let's speak on that?" Meech fumed and wanted to get in his ass some more.

"Yeah, that right there is mine you violated," Meech growled. "Don't believe that bullshit, Zeneka." Meech saw the hurt in Zeneka's eyes. Zeneka was confused after Rozay's accusations. She just wanted them both out of her life. Meech was pissed off, but he knew it was best to leave although he didn't want to. Aggravated that he couldn't finish what he had started he spat, "Fuck this. I'm out of here."

"Oh, yeah, pretty boy. This not over. Your ass is mine," Meech fumed as he left just as quickly as he had come.

Zeneka, still in shock with her mouth covered, watched a battered Rozay dust himself off. He looked at Zeneka like she had set him up.

"That's fucked up. You set me up," a pissed off Rozay spat.

"I didn't know he was going to show up," Zeneka snapped.

"Whatever, he got me, but payback's a bitch," Rozay whined.

"So, why did you throw Zeneka at him?" Zeneka questioned

"I heard you loud and clear, believe me," Rozay scowled, embarrassed as he walked off. "Ask your husband bout him and Zania."

"A word of caution before you plot some revenge, you better ask around about the Barksdale family," Zeneka advised before she walked away.

Rozay didn't respond, he just kept walking. Zeneka pulled out her phone to call Shanice to tell her what had happened.

Shanice answered, "What the hell is going on?"

"Rozay had been harassing me for a while, so I agreed to meet him," Zeneka responded.

"Girl, stop," Shanice cooed.

Zeneka shot a dead ass serious look at the phone.

"I'm so sorry. I've never experienced that side of him," Shanice responded. "He left that part out when he just called. He just said Meech jumped him and beat his ass."

Zeneka giggled then cooed, "Yeah, that part is true. He just popped up out of nowhere and commenced to beating Rozay's ass."

"That's what his ass gets," Shanice added.

"Plus, with what happened to Lucci, Meech's ass is in straight savage mode. Shit scared the hell out of me," Zeneka whined.

"So, Meech fucked him up?" Shanice asked.

"Girl, yeah, he said Rozay was fucking with what was his," Zeneka sighed.

"Well, I see his point. You lucky he didn't fuck you up also," Shanice teased.

Zeneka giggled again, "Believe me, a bitch was scared."

"That nigga a Barksdale. Tread lightly," Shanice advised.

"Hell, your ass carrying one of those crazy fuckers," Zeneka joked.

"I will fuck his or her little ass up if they acted like them," Shanice threatened.

Zeneka burst into laughter then said, "I'm late for my class. See you at dinner." She ended the call abruptly.

After a long day of loud kids and crazy men, Zeneka was excited about seeing Shanice, plus, she was as hungry as a hostage. Her lunch break was filled with Meech's shenanigans, but he did, in a crazy way, help her, hopefully, get through to Rozay. As soon as Zeneka walked in, the aroma of the seasons flowed from the kitchen. *"Damn, it smells good in here,"* she thought to herself as she surveyed the restaurant. Shanice was drying her hands coming out of the restroom. Zeneka looked at her gas-faced, "Ewww. We using public restrooms now?"

Shanice side-eyed her back, then joked, "It's this damn demon-seed in me."

"Aight, watch your mouth that's my godson," Zeneka shot back as they searched for a table. Shanice just smirked as they took their seats. She wasn't about to reveal Rozay's accusation to Shanice till she got with Meech and Zeneka.

***

Zeneka and Shanice were looking at the menu for China Express for lunch.

"How are doing girl?" Zeneka asked knowing that Shanice was going through it with Lucci. So, she didn't want to talk about her men problems.

"I'm okay, just ready for them to move Lucci out of I.C.U," answered Shanice.

Silence fell between them but Zeneka said, "He's the better of the brothers he will be a great father."

Shanice's stress seemed to visibly disappear at her statement. "Dry those tears mommy. You don't need to be getting upset," cheered Zeneka. "Enough of all that, what are you ordering?" Zeneka said handing her a napkin. The waitress was standing tableside waiting on their order.

Cracking a faint smile and feeling more assured Shanice said, "Beef and Broccoli with garlic rice."

"All that garlic, you're gonna have the dragon in your mouth," joked Zeneka trying to cheer her up.

Shanice burst out into laughter and said, "You know your ass stupid, right?"

While giggling uncontrollably, Zeneka said, "Cause you're

my boo." They both were stuffed, had enjoyed each other's company. Thirty minutes later they were standing by their cars.

"I'm so sleepy right now," yawned Shanice.

"Go your pregnant ass home, get some rest," joked Zeneka.

"I can't, I'm on a case for your in-laws," she answered.

"So glad those days are over," smiled Zeneka.

"Well, they have been generous to me over the years so I can't co-sign," responded Shanice.

"I didn't mean it like that. I mean materialistically, Meech took care of me. But emotionally, he wrecked me," sighed Zeneka.

"I knew what you meant, girl," cooed Shanice. "Well, call me later, I got to get back," Zeneka said as she looked at her watch. "Okay, boo. I will call you later," Shanice said.

***

Zania was hung over. She had called off work thinking about the confrontation with Rozay. She knew that time was of the essence with Rozay showing his unstable side. She also reflected on the night of pleasure they shared. Never had she climaxed so much in her life, but the crazy attached to it wasn't worth it. She had to tell Zeneka about Meech being Javon's father. Meech was at the top of her list. She needed to give him a call soon as she got her hangover headache stabilized.

Javon was with her parents, so she was free to do whatever she wanted. She hadn't hung with her girl, Cashmere, in a while. She picked her phone up and dialed Cashmere's number.

"Hey, bitch where you been hiding?" Cashmere teased.

Zania smiled then said, "I been around. I'm childless, wassup?"

"Hell, you already know it's a turn-up," Cashmere laughed.

"Those niggas better watch out. We're coming to clean their asses out," Zania co-signed.

"Okay, so let's meet at Labels in the Music Factory. I heard ballers be in there strong."

"Cash in the house, heey," Cashmere chimed.

"Girl, bye," Zania laughed as they ended the call.

She looked at the clock. It was 8:07. She hurried to the shower because she wanted to get there early.

Hours later, after waiting in line for twenty minutes, Zania was finally inside a crowded Labels. She made her way to an empty table at the back of the club. Minutes later, Cashmere was coming through the crowd.

"Hey, chica, wassup?" Cashmere smiled.

"Damn, this place is packed," Zania said.

Zania frowned then said, "Let's go to Bar One instead. I don't want none of these sweaty, broke ass niggas up against my Gucci."

"I feel you. These niggas do look broke," Cashmere joked. She side-eyed a guy with a wrinkled suit as they made their way to the exit.

"Girl, your ass crazy," Zania giggled.

Twenty minutes later they arrived at Bar One on North

College Street. Bar One was a red brick, two-story building. The bouncer was even friendlier, it was more upscale. "Yesss, bitch, this our type of place," Cashmere snapped as they entered the lounge.

The bar was littered with well-dressed men. The inside décor was red faux brick with tied, white drapes, and it was well-lit. The bar was a cherry, mahogany oak with a black bottom. The club was spacious. As they sat at their table, they were greeted by a waitress.

"What are you ladies drinking?" she welcomed.

She read off the house specials, and they both agreed on Apple martinis.

"Look at all these ballers for the picking," Cashmere laughed.

As Zania was scanning the room, she saw Meech in the VIP area with a woman whose back was turned to her.

"His sorry ass," she said under her breath. Cashmere was so engrossed in the scenery that she didn't hear her.

"Ladies, here's your drinks," the waitress said.

They grabbed their drinks off her platter.

"That will be seventeen dollars," the waitress said as she started to give Zania her change from the twenty.

"Keep it the change sweetie, and keep them coming," Zania said.

"Yes, ma'am," the waitress obliged.

Cashmere was eyeing a dark-skinned guy at the bar who was dressed in all black slacks with a black dress shirt and long dreads.

"Damn, he fine. I gotta have him," Cashmere yelped as she eyeballed the stranger. "Why you eye fucking that nigga in the corner?" Cashmere hissed.

"That's Javon's father," Zania admitted as she debated whether to blast him. Cashmere's mouth dropped because she remembered Meech from the club, but she didn't give any details to Zania.

"GGGGirl, I know that dude. Me and Mesha hooked up with him and his brother Lucci," Cashmere smiled.

Zania scrunched her face then fumed, "That's nothing new. Both of them are trifling ass dogs. They run through women like water."

Mesha said smirking, "Meech fucked her good."

"I know he ain't shit," Zania snapped. Zania was pissed. In her mind, Meech's dick belonged to her. Cashmere stood up to go terrorize her victim at the bar.

"Girl, let me see what this nigga pockets about," Cashmere teased while chewing on a straw.

***

Meech frowned because he knew his peace was about to leave. "Damn, Zania sorry ass done spotted me. A nigga was trying to relax, but I know she going to be on some petty shit," he sighed. "I can tell those hoes talking about me the way she keeps peeping over here. Hindsight is twenty-twenty. If she comes over here on some rah-rah shit, I'm going to crack her face like a mirror. Her dumb ass just don't know. Now is not the time to fuck with a nigga. I got mad pressure on me. I will explode on her ass. I've been kicking this

Hennessy back all night, so it won't be good for her to fuck with me tonight.

***

*Z*ania...

"*His ass sat back in the cut, chilling. Let me fuck up his night. These bitches riding his dick like an elevator, while he being stingy with me when it comes to the dick. He going to make me fuck him up,*" Zania thought to herself. She knew she was about to blast his ass for not spending more time with their son. He and Zeneka were getting a divorce, but she just wanted to be petty, piss him off. He was looking too happy. Plus, the way Rozay crazy ass murdered her pussy, she was good on dick. She walked back there to fuck with him.

Zania strolled over to the VIP, where her and Meech's eyes locked. She saw him as he sighed. The club bouncer blocked the entranceway.

"I have someone I need to talk to in VIP," Zania popped off.

"Little mama, you're not allowed up here," the bouncer frowned.

"Meech, I know you see me!" Zania yelled. Meech smiled and dropped his head.

The bouncer looked in Meech's direction who was sitting by himself smoking a cigar smiling.

Zania was trying to push past the bouncer.

"Your son wants to see your punk ass!" Zania yelled.

"C'mon, baby girl, don't do this," the bouncer responded.

Her being belligerent got Meech's attention, and he signaled for the bouncer to let her through.

"Now, what is it that I can do for your messy ass," Meech teased as Zania sat down. "I gave you entrance. I didn't tell you to sit, but this won't take long. I was sitting here wondering how I was gonna do this, then your messy, shade throwing ass popped up ruining my evening. So, I might as well ruin yours," Meech smiled.

Zania gave a dismal look at his verbal assassination of her character.

"I think you will want to see this," he smiled as he handed her a certified envelope.

She ripped the envelope open, and her mouth fell open as her eyes widened.

"Chances of paternity, zero point zero zero," she read slowly.

"When did you do this?" she questioned.

"Last time I had Javon, I swabbed him," Meech smiled. "NOT THE FATHER..."

"Believe me, this shit not done," Zania snapped.

Everyone in the VIP cheered as she slowly stood and walked away. He had the DJ to play Usher's song, "Let It Burn." The tables next to him cheered, "NOT THE FATHER!"

"Get your trifling ass out of here," he clowned.

Zania was humiliated because in her mind, she was innocent. "You will be lucky if I don't put your ass out of my house. Better yet, you better hope I don't make your ass start paying rent," Meech laughed.

"Drinks on me," he told the other patrons as he stood holding his glass in the air. Zania was walking at a steady pace trying to leave as her tears flowed uncontrollably. Cashmere saw her near the front of the club and stepped in front of her.

"What's wrong? Why are you leaving?" Cashmere pried.

"Yeah, you know how niggas be tripping," Zania lied. Cashmere knew niggas like Meech held a low regard for women, so she could formulate what had happened.

Sniffling, drying her tears she lied, "It's late and my mom dropping my son off in the morning."

Zania made a quick exit glad that the front part of the club didn't see Meech embarrass her.

Cashmere didn't want to lose her baller she had on the hook said, "Okay, baby girl text me when you get home."

"Okay, I will," she responded as she walked off.

Minutes later, Zania knew that the privileged life that came from Meech's secret funding was ended. She could no longer blackmail him. She knew she would feel the wrath of his vindictiveness. Zania always thought Meech was the father. Emotionally crushed by the one man who was just as malicious as her. Tears poured uncontrollably as she drove home, she was entrenched in thought as the melody of Mary J. Blige, "I'm Not Gonna Cry" filled the cabin of the Suburban of that Meech had purchased six months ago.

I guess karma's a bitch. I'm fucked up right now, my head is definitely in a bad place right now. He truly cracked my face. I can't believe he's not the father of my son Javon. The look on his face was full of hate and aggravation. I have cause so much hurt and pain over the years. I was always treated second-class to Zeneka by everyone that was the fuel for my pain. I knew that Meech was the one thing she truly loved ever since we were younger. I know it's trifling but I don't give a fuck. This pain and hurt will pass.

****

A month later......
Lucci had been in a private room for three days, and he hadn't had any visitors for a few days. Shanice was going to visit, but he told her of his plan to leave. He told her he would explain later when they met up, and she obliged. Lucci knew he had thirty minutes to escape between nurses changing shifts. So, he conned a nurse to bring him some clothes.

After ten minutes of struggling to dress, he hobbled to the freight elevator. Lucci had finally made it out of the hospital. He was still bandaged, but overall, he was intact. He made his way down the walkway that led to the bus stop. He sat down in the bus depot, which reeked of piss and stinking asses that had occupied the seat before. Lucci had known before it was all said and done that he would have to kill his lifelong friend. He knew that the Barksdale's would lose street cred if he didn't balance the scales, and he wasn't having that.

The bus finally arrived. Lucci sat at the back of the bus, so he wouldn't draw attention to himself. The bus was quickly packed with people coming from the hospital or workers. Lucci slid in the corner and put his head down the whole ride, hoping not to be noticed.

The bus ride was thirty minutes in, and Lucci was almost at his destination when he saw a familiar face. He positioned his face in his hoodie, to go unnoticed as Willie, the neighborhood crackhead, mechanic, and jack-of-all-trades, approached him smelling like old pussy and musty balls.

He had on a polo shirt that was once white, but now shit brown and his jeans were baggy, wrinkled, and had dirt stains all on them.

He stumbled down the aisle, grabbing all the railing along the way. His body odor arrived before him. Lucci was relieved when he sat in a seat midways on the bus. His back was to Lucci. Lucci hit the button for the next stop. He knew he was a few blocks from his destination, but he would rather walk than let Willie see him because that was the neighborhood snitch.

Lucci quickly rose up from the seat and exited the bus as Willie turned to see who was getting off.

Fifteen minutes later, he was crashing on a wide, green suede type of couch in the living room, which looked as if it designed by a top-notch interior decorator. The walls were brilliant earth tones, accented in coppers and multiple shades of brown. His furniture was all Bassett with Bob Timberlake paintings on the walls. It was a house that the family had given to him.

The floor was Italian marble. The room overall was spacious, fitting an executive, not a thug like Lucci. His 60-inch flat screen came out of the ceiling. Lucci's body ached from the bus trip and walk. He dozed off from the exhaustion in the comfort of his home.

Lucci was awakened by the neighbors' sex session next door. He sat up on the couch strategizing what he would need to do to exact his revenge. The ideas played in his mind like a movie. He also knew he would have to make a move quickly because he knew his family and detectives would be looking to talk to him.

Lucci had a hideaway place on the outskirts of Huntersville. He knew he had to get to his stash spot for survival. He would make his move in a few days once his body adjusted to being without medication. His body ached for medication, but he was going to wean himself off of it.

He laid back on the couch, and sleep took over quickly. Morning came quicker than he wished for as his body called out for medication. He wasn't having any of that, he thought to himself. The last thing he needed was a new addiction while trying to focus on his plan of attack. His stomach growled as he sat contemplating his next move.

Thirty-minutes later, he had eaten and hobbled around trying to get prepped for a shower. Five minutes later, he was undressed and looking at his scars. Removing bandages, he flinched as the adhesive stuck to his skin. "What the fuck?" he whined as the pain throbbed with every pull. The gauze left remnants on his skin.

Lucci reached into the shower to turn it on. The water was piping hot as he stepped in. Ten minutes later, he was drying off so he could re-bandage his wounds and get ready for his mission to get to his hideaway spot. He would need to reach out to Shanice to get to his destination. Lucci got dressed as quickly as he could before he called her, making sure to put on a bulletproof vest while doing so. He knew to travel lightly.

He went to the guest bedroom and removed the mounted flat screen. It revealed a safe with stacks of cash inside, which he knew they would need to reach his destination. He knew to only use secure contacts. He would have to think awhile before mapping out their getaway.

Lucci clicked on the television to catch the latter half of the game as he propped his leg. He got himself comfortable as he laid out on the King Edward couch with the extended ottoman. He could almost get lost in it. He felt like a king sitting on his throne the way the couch sat high. His body was calling for rest, which was becoming a handicap for him. He knew he needed to reach out to Shanice because she was the only person he trusted. He would call her once he had his daily nap.

Lucci drifted off into a deep sleep. He tossed and turned in his sleep as the dreams of being shot played in his head. He was drenched in a cold sweat. He was slightly hysterical when he first awoke, but he regained his composure quickly. Lucci sat up, maneuvered to the edge of the couch, and reached for a glass of water that was sitting on the table. The sip relaxed him. This situation had really taken a toll on him and made him feel like he was missing a part of himself, but he already knew in his mind what he had to do, regardless. His first priority was to get to what he considered his safe zone. His mind really fucked with him, and his body ached for drugs, but he just bore the pain.

As he was dozed off, he heard the doorknob turn. *Who the fuck is this,* he thought as he scrambled for his gun. He grabbed his .45. "Who the fuck is it?" he yelled as his adrenaline rushed. He heard heels clicking.

"It's me, escapee," Shanice snapped. Lucci relaxed at the sight of Shanice. "So, what's the plan?" Shanice joked as a tear ran down her cheek.

Lucci took her hand and wiped her tears, surprised at her reaction. "Hey, what's wrong?" he asked as he pulled her closer.

Shanice whined, "We need you here," she smiled at a puzzled Lucci.

"Well, I know my fam got my back," Lucci answered.

Shanice tenderly rubbed his face while looking in his eyes said, "No, we need you here," while placing his hand on her stomach. "Oh, shit we have a baby," he said clapping his hands.

"So, you're okay with me being pregnant?" a surprised Shanice asked.

"Come here," Lucci motioned. "I'm not going anywhere. I got y'all. Do you need anything?" Lucci asked.

"No, bae. Everything I needed, you just gave me," Shanice beamed. Shanice laid across Lucci's lap as he caressed her. "Sooo, babe, does your family know you left the hospital?" Shanice smiled.

Hesitant to answer he said, "No, not yet. I will tell them. I don't need them worrying, jumping to conclusions, and start fucking people up."

"So, why did you leave?" Shanice snapped.

"I wasn't going to give a motherfucker a chance to finish me off," Lucci fumed as he rubbed Shanice's stomach. "Are you up for a getaway?"

Shanice smiled at his offer, "Sure, I need a getaway. Let me call my secretary and leave orders for my paralegals."

"Aight, we get packed up tonight," Lucci said.

"Well, bae, I gotta get back to work, but I will go home pack and come back," Shanice confirmed. Lucci stood to walk her out. He grabbed her and pressed his lips against hers. Shanice accepted his tongue as his hands freely roamed her backside. "Bae, I will be back," Shanice said and pried herself away. "Call your people," she chimed.

"I will. You not the boss of me," Lucci joked, still excited about the news of the pregnancy.

"Nope, but your family is," Shanice giggled. Shanice closed the door behind her.

Minutes later, Lucci was calling Meech. "Wassup, bruh?" Lucci questioned.

Meech looked at his phone. He knew it was Lucci's number, but he was looking at his phone like he was being pranked. "Who the fuck is this?" Meech snapped.

"This me, bruh. I left the hospital," Lucci confirmed.

"No shit. I'm sorry I haven't been there like I should've been. Absalom has had me stretched out with all these shipments. Plus, I'm trying to dead this divorce."

"It's cool. Just giving the family a heads up in case y'all went by the hospital," Lucci added.

"Are you good though?" a concerned Meech asked.

"Yes, I'm good. Oh, yeah, we having a baby," Lucci huffed.

"Congratulations, little brother," Meech beamed. "I just blasted Zeneka's ass last night. Javon's not mine. I swabbed him and showed her scandalous ass the results."

Lucci burst out in laughter at Meech's words. "She so fucking messy. I'm glad you blasted her whorish ass."

"That bitch better go to the Maury show," they both chimed.

"Aight bruh, I'm headed to this divorce meeting," Meech ended.

"Hit me up later, bruh," Lucci said ending the call.

***

"I apologize for my lateness," Meech said as he walked into the boardroom where Zeneka and a paralegal were sitting.

"You're pardoned. We are just looking over the property division papers," the paralegal said.

"Whatever she wants, give it to her," Meech scoffed. "You looking good these days," he said as he signed the papers.

"So, just like that. I guess you never did love me," Zeneka whined.

Meech listened to her statement then spat, "No, I did my dirt, but you stopped being my wife when you fucked someone else in our house."

Zeneka was shocked at his allegations, but she knew he was telling the truth. Tears welled in her eyes, "I can't argue that. I just wanted revenge."

The paralegal listened to the words being slung then said, "Well, our business here is done. I will file these today."

Meech stood up and said, "Take care of yourself. I'm outta here."

Everyone left the boardroom as Zeneka dropped her head to the table as tears flowed. Jamari was just a distraction. In her heart, she wanted Meech to fight for their marriage. She stood, wiped her eyes, and she left out of the boardroom.

****

Zeneka and Jamari were on their way to dinner.

"Are you going to give me the silent treatment all evening?" Jamari smiled.

"No, just have a lot on my mind. I apologize for being a stick in the mud," she sulked.

Jamari knew that she was still in her feelings about her divorce. "You're acting like you mind because he gave you what you asked for," Jamari chimed. Zeneka looked out the window at her response.

"I guess I expected him to fight for us," Zeneka answered.

Her response stung his ego and slightly pissed him off. "What the hell? Did you forget he's fucking my sister?" Jamari fumed.

Zeneka knew her mindset was fucked up, and her intent wasn't to hurt him. "Can we just drop it?" Zeneka snapped.

Jamari laughed, "I guess the truth does hurt. You acting holier than thou. Man, please, I know you confused," Jamari smirked.

Zeneka sighed, "I'm not feeling you and the fact that you're all in your feelings."

Jamari, slightly aggravated, snapped, "Let me take your ass home. When you're done with the pity party hit me up."

"Yeah, just take me home," Zeneka said.

****

Lucci was packed and ready to ride out. He felt better. His body was at eighty percent as he waited patiently for Shanice to arrive at his destination. He had decided that he would get Shanice to take him. She was always down for him regardless of the situation. She was a true ride or die, thick or thin type of chick. He hated that he hadn't treated her right in the beginning and was carrying his baby, he knew they needed some away time.

At eight-thirty, Shanice pulled up the driveway in a black Mercedes truck with dark tinted windows. She stepped out wearing a pair of Manolo pumps, and a blue, fitted dress that always accentuated her wide, bubbled ass and small waist. She had a face that reminded you of Diahann Carroll, and she always sported a vertical, bob cut.

Lucci was peeking out of the window as she exited the truck. Her beauty had him entranced as she walked like a refined model walking a runway. When she tapped lightly on the door, it caught him off guard.

She saw him peeking out at her, "Are you gonna let me in?" she joked.

"Hold on, I'm coming," he answered back. He swung the door open, as they embraced each other his hand grazed her ass.

"For a sick man, you're looking mighty fresh," Shanice remarked.

Lucci released her and said, "You know that ass has a mind of its own."

They both took each other in. As the conversation flowed, they felt the sexual tension building.

"So, how are you feeling?" she asked Lucci.

His head dropped when she made that statement and remarked," Yeah, just glad to get away."

"Me too, because I want my baby to have both parents," she assured him.

The room went silent after her statement, and then Lucci said, "I'm open to that."

"Enough about that, babe. Where are you headed?" she inquired.

"We are going to fall off the earth," he answered, and she knew exactly what he meant.

She smiled because he knew she always loved his getaway spot. "Why you smiling so hard?" he joked. She poked him as he did so. Lucci grabbed his bags as they headed to the door to start their journey.

Shanice was all smiles as Lucci rested in the passenger seat. She bopped her head to some old school Mary J. Blige that was playing on the radio. Her automated GPS told her she was about forty-five minutes from their destination, which made her even more excited. That spot had always been special to her for the fact that Lucci had only shared his getaway spot with her, plus the memories they had made there. It was the middle of the winter, so she knew the scenery would be beautiful.

Lucci was talking in his sleep, but she couldn't make out exactly what he was saying so she didn't get alarmed. She was ten minutes from her destination. She tapped Lucci to wake him, and he woke up with a frown on his face.

As he wiped his face, he looked out the window and saw the snow-covered ground. Lucci's face lit up as he took in the scenery. It was a new world compared to the concrete city. The pine trees were snow-covered, and everything was spaced out, unlike the cramped city. The mountainous scenery was snowcapped like something from a postcard.

"Do you see how beautiful it is up here?" Shanice said smiling at Lucci who was staring out the window.

He was just as excited. He just didn't show it. His mind

was finally tranquil and at peace. He was no longer focused on the events that had transpired. He was focused on catching up with Shanice and would deal with the other stuff at the appropriate time. Lucci finally answered, "Yeah, it's nice up here."

Shanice knew him. She knew he was in a good state of mind, so he could focus on his recovery. "We need this. The other shit we will deal with at the right time," Shanice said as though she had read his mind. Lucci just stared at her as he laughed to himself. Shanice had always found his smile sexy.

Lucci was coming around as the scenery became more enchanting by the snowcapped hills. His ranch-styled home was covered with snow, and the walkways were glazed with ice. The house was gray with shutters, and it had a sunroom that revealed a room full of gray furniture. Shanice pulled into the icy driveway and parked. The ice still crunched after the car came to a rest. "Well, we are finally here," Shanice smiled.

"Are you happy now?" Lucci asked as he opened the car door. He knew he had to be careful stepping down on the slick ice in his condition. Shanice knew she would have to help him, so she replaced her heels with some Nike's she had in the back. "Hold on, let me come help you. This ice is slippery," Shanice commanded.

"What, you think I'm a cripple?" Lucci snapped.

Shanice was taken aback by his response, "What the fuck you tripping about? Did I call you crippled?" she fired back.

Lucci slumped back in the seat knowing she was speaking the truth. Lucci was looking out the bay window of the living room as Shanice was unpacking their bags, his mind was finally at ease from the shooting that had taken place. Still in disbelief, he blocked it out of his mind and watched the local news. He knew that the police would be looking to question him seeing that he had left the hospital. He also knew he had to figure out who shot him and kill them. That was the creed of the street. "I hope you not still letting that bullshit flood your mind," Shanice coached.

Lucci just sank back in his seat, mind still in fast-forward as Shanice massaged his shoulders to relax him. Lucci was always comfortable around Shanice. "Are you hungry?" Shanice asked. "Do you need to take any medications, because that was a long ride? I know it was hard on your body," she inquired.

"I'm good. I appreciate the concern," he responded as he placed his hands over hers. She was the only one he allowed to see his gentle side. In the streets, he was regarded as a monster; but to Shanice, he was just Little Lucci. "So, what are we going to do to kill time?" Shanice asked in a flirting manner. Lucci's eyes widened at her innuendo. It had been awhile since he had sex.

"We could also catch a game on television," he interjected. Shanice's spirits were crushed by his remark. She was expecting a romantic getaway.

"Well, it won't be any game watching in here," Shanice stated as she swooped in to grab the remote. "We watching Love & Hip-Hop Atlanta," Shanice smiled. Lucci looked surprised as she stood back with her hands on her hips. She walked forward toward him as he sunk back in the chair. She placed her hands on his knees and leaned her face until her lips pressed against his and slid her tongue into his mouth. He was now pushing forward. As he leaned forward, he wrapped his hands around her waist as they made her way to her round behind to pull her into him.

He pulled away and asked her, "Are you sure you're ready for this?" Shanice just stared at Lucci's vulnerability. It was sad to say, but it was like the shooting gave him a new outlook.

"I told you I'm nobody's baby momma," she confessed.

****

Zania was slumped over the arm of her sofa as Zeneka let herself in. "What the fuck?" she gasped at a drunken Zania. "Hey, you didn't work today?" Zeneka asked a half comatose Zania. Zeneka shook her head at the living room littered with liquor bottles. "Wake your ass up," Zeneka shook her.

"WWhat?" Zania snapped as she looked disheveled in a stained house robe. Her house was a mess. "What you doing in my house?" she fumed. She stood up and pointed her finger at Zeneka. "You're the problem. Everyone loves you and treat me like I'm shit," she whined as tears ran down her cheeks. Her speech was slurred as she regained her composure.

"Baby girl, I'm not a threat to you. You're my sister," Zeneka assured her.

"I got that crazy ass Rozay blackmailing me behind your ass," Zania sobbed.

"What is he blackmailing you for? And when did y'all get tight like that?" Zeneka pried.

"He's obsessed with you," Zania cried.

"So how is he blackmailing you?" Zeneka asked.

Zania dropped her head and spat, "He tried to say me and Meech were sleeping together."

Zeneka sat stunned at what she said. "I know I didn't hear what you said correctly," Zeneka spat. "Why the hell would he think that, Zania?" She watched as Zania started fidgeting with the button on her housecoat.

"Now, Zeneka, you know that motherfucker crazy," she answered.

Zeneka was now rocking her leg, as her sister's words resonated through her head. "Call him," Zeneka snapped.

Zeneka's response caught Zania off-guard. "Huh, call who? Why you can't take my word for it?" Zania pleaded as her eyes widened.

Zeneka could tell by Zania mannerisms and change in demeanor that she was lying. Zeneka's heart was hurting like Zania had stabbed her with several knives. She leaped up from her seat, and her right hand smacked the spittle from Zania mouth. "OOOO, bitch, no you didn't do no grimy shit like that to me," Zeneka fumed while connecting a left hook to Zania's jaw that knocked her on the couch and her mouth leaking blood.

Zania's attempt to retaliate was futile. Her being hungover didn't help her defense. "Zeneka, what the fuck?" she muttered as Zeneka mushed her head and grabbed her purse.

"You want to fuck my husband, you're dead to me and I got you," Zeneka frowned as she drew back to hit her again.

"Bitch, you not worth it," she said as she walked out. "Bitch, I wish you would call the police. I will come back and really fuck you up. Believe, I'm not done." Zeneka wiped her tears after she closed the door.

Of all the shit Meech had done, this was one she could never fathom. What, when, how, ran through her head as she headed towards Meech's new house. She was going to call, but she wanted to pop up. She made her way up the freshly paved driveway and saw his new Cadillac Escalade as she got closer. She was impressed by the gray Colonial-style house with white columns and freshly manicured lawn. *"I be damned," escaped her lips. "That's why his ass was so generous. Son of a bitch."* Just as she was about to park, Meech was coming out wearing a dark, denim Levi jeans set with blue Timberlands and a black Lacoste button-down. Zeneka stepped out of her gray Camaro.

"How did you know where I live?" smirked a surprised Meech.

Avoiding his question, Zeneka spat, "So you fucked my messy ass sister?"

Meech quickly got defensive, "Remember, we're not married anymore."

Zeneka rolled her eyes at his answer then said, "Were you trying to break me?" Zeneka yelled. Tears flowed like the river as Meech stood stone-faced.

"It was a mistake, Zeneka, we hit a rough patch," he answered.

WHAP! Before he could lie to her anymore, she sucker

punched him. Meech stepped back as she tried to hit him again and he grabbed her hand. "Neither one of y'all are shit," she hissed as he blocked her punches.

"Aight, I don't hit women, but I'm about to knock your ass out," Meech smirked.

"You ain't shit. Damn sure not worth my time," she said as she tried to kick him.

"You best get in that little car of yours, enjoy the life I gave you," an irritated Meech yelled. "Now get the fuck out of my way so I can go check on my brother," an irritated Meech said. Heartbroken and betrayed, Zeneka walked back to her car defeated. As she revved her engine up, she thought about running Meech's ass over, but figured he wasn't worth it. "Go enjoy that life I just gave you," Meech teased as he inspected himself for scars.

****

Shanice's body was receptive to his touch as she moaned, "Baby, hold on," she whispered as she unbuttoned her dress which revealed perfectly rounded C-cup breasts, held in by a blue, Victoria Secret bra. As her dress fell to the floor, it revealed a tight, caramel-skinned ass in blue, matching thongs.

"Damn, baby, your body still tight like it was when we were younger," he murmured.

Lucci hovered over her. As he leaned in to kiss her, she enveloped his tongue. His hands roamed over her ass as she pressed against his erect dick. Her hand roamed to cup it through his jeans as she tugged at his zipper to free his dick.

She stroked it fiercely as he bucked with every stroke. His dick was fully erect, but her hand wasn't big enough to encompass it. His jeans fell to the floor. She straddled him, and he fell back on the couch. Her pussy expanded as she plunged down hard.

"Oh damn," she moaned as he delved deep in her saturated pussy, which was leaking on his thighs. Her head rested on his shoulder as he lifted her up. With her in tow, he deep stroked her pussy like a man with no abandonment. She moaned loudly as he hoisted her into the air, meeting every deep stroke.

"Oh damn, Oh shit," she murmured.

He let out a loud yelp as he exploded inside her pussy walls and collapsed back onto the couch, Shanice smiled and said, "You seemed pretty healthy to me."

Lucci just smiled and said, "It's not my best work, but long as you're satisfied."

"Well, I'm assuming dinner's ready," she chuckled as she jumped off him and made her way to the kitchen.

"So, is it ready? Do you know what you doing?"

"Shut up boy," she retorted. Shanice liked how their little session had changed his mindset. He was back to being himself. He seemed at ease.

Lucci was now focused on the game again as Shanice worked her magic in the kitchen. When a round of shots let off, Lucci jumped and ran towards the kitchen and pushed Shanice to the floor. The shots echoed in the background. Shanice's face wore a panicked look as Lucci covered her to shelter her from danger. "Stay down till I tell you it's clear," he yelled. Lucci scurried to a window to see what was going on.

Shanice, being around Lucci, wasn't scared. She was used to that life. "Lucci, be careful," she yelled across the room. Lucci was now checking the window as he pulled his forty-five from the back of his jeans.

"Where the hell did that come from?" Shanice asked. She was flashing as Lucci looked back at her in shock, but he already knew Shanice was always ready for whatever.

"Where the hell did you have that hiding?" he yelled back to Shanice. Lucci was now eye level with the window as he pulled the curtains back to see what was going on. He cracked the door not to be noticeable. It was some kids with some homemade fireworks. He looked back to signal to Shanice, it was a false alarm.

"Are you okay?" she asked him. Sweat glistened from Lucci's face at the false alarm. His rapid change in breathing had slowed down. "Whew," Shanice sighed, as she made her way back to the stove to check on the food. Lucci had returned to his game. Shanice noticed how Lucci's demeanor had changed back so quickly. "You looked a little rusty there, old man," Shanice joked.

Lucci just fanned away her comments then said, "My skills are still on point."

Shanice liked the fact that the false alarm didn't make him revert back to how he was before. "After all that, have you worked up an appetite?" she asked as she pulled two plates from the cabinet.

"I guess I'm ready to taste this food you have made," he joked. Lucci got up to make his way to the bathroom to wash his hands.

"Least you know to wash your hands," she teased as she followed suit. Five minutes later, they were eating, reminiscing, and enjoying each other's company. "Check the guide; see if any good movies on," Shanice said as she cleared the table of the dinner dishes.

Shanice had always wanted to be Lucci's wife, but she always knew in the back of her mind that he would always be in love with the street life. She knew to just enjoy the time while she could.

"So, what are you thinking?" she asked as she pulled a pie from the oven.

"Well, I'm just reflecting on some of the dumb shit I have been through in my life," he laughed as he shook his head.

"Well, I'm going to have to agree with you on that," she laughed. "But you're crazy ass always got out of them."

"Yeah, I must have had an angel on my shoulder or some shit," he laughed as he took a bite of pie.

"I believe you had a horseshoe up your butt," she added. "I prayed for you a many of days."

Shanice felt herself getting emotional at the thought of Lucci not being around, a thought she hated to even fathom.

About that time, there was a tap at the door. Lucci's body tensed up again as the tap became more rapid. Shanice walked towards the door with her 9mm in hand. She couldn't make out the figure at the door, so she jerked the door open with gun drawn, "Who the fuck is you?"

The tall, dark-skinned man threw his hands up in surrender and smoothly said, "I work for the Barksdale's."

Lucci tucked his gun back into the back of his shirt. Relieved he said, "Where is he and how did he know where to find me?" he demanded. Shanice still stayed cocked and loaded as the man looked away.

Making no sudden moves, he again spoke, "He's still in the car. I was just doing what I was told."

Lucci had now made his way to the door to look at the dark, tinted Escalade that was parked in front of the house. Shanice eased her grip on the 9mm.

"Well don't stand your ass there, tell him to come in," Lucci anxiously said as he pushed past Shanice and the chauffeur to make it to his Escalade to greet Meech.

Meech had now stepped out of the car to greet Lucci. Shanice watched as Lucci's demeanor changed as he greeted his brother with a quick embrace. "What the hell you doing here?" Lucci asked smiling like a kid at Christmas time.

"My little brother, why wouldn't I keep an eye on you," Meech answered jokingly. Shanice was happy to see Meech. Meech was draped in a cream, linen pants suit with a matching fur Kangol brim and suede, mocha Timberlands.

"What the fuck is going on?" Meech inquired. "Are you losing your touch?"

Lucci leaned against the Escalade with his arms folded and responded, "Naw, I just was having a bad day that's all. So, what brings you this way besides you being nosey?" Lucci inquired.

Meech rubbed his brow at the question, "You know I got to always check on my little brother," he laughed. "That's my job to have your back and you have mine." They dapped each other up and nodded in agreeance. Shanice smiled as they interacted.

"So, how long y'all going to be here?" Meech asked as his tone turned serious.

Lucci stood silently as if he was pondering the question and answered, "Not sure yet."

Meech nodded his head and said, "You know we got to set a trap for this rat."

They both made their way towards the house where Shanice was. She shouted down the porch stairs, "Barksdale's in full effect," she teased. They both smiled as they neared her and the top of the stairs.

"Shanice, how are you?" Meech asked and embraced her.

"Let me go fool," she said laughing, glad to see him.

"I see I'm going to be an uncle," he shot back at Shanice. Shanice just rolled her eyes at his comment. "Charles, you can go back to the car," Meech said as he walked past him.

The driver seemed relieved by his orders. "Yes sir," was all that escaped the chauffeur's lips as he cleared the steps at a swift pace.

Meech pulled Shanice's shirt as he walked by her and joked, "Don't be pulling no guns on my damn driver." Lucci laughed at him harassing Shanice as they made their way into the house.

"Meech, you want something to eat?" Shanice asked, who was in wife-to-be mode.

"What you cook Shanice?" he asked. She ran the menu down to him, and he accepted. She piled his plate with chicken, sweet potatoes, and macaroni & cheese. Meech's eyes widened when he saw the plate. His mouth watered as Shanice sat the plate before him. "Who really cooked this?" he joked.

Twenty minutes later, Lucci and Meech were at the table talking when Shanice interrupted, "How did the divorce proceeding go?"

Meech answered, "I gave her everything she asked for."

Shanice sighed, "I should've been there for her."

"She confronted me about Zania and Javon," a deflated Meech said.

"What the fuck? How did she find out?" an annoyed Shanice questioned. "Excuse me, I've got to call her," a concerned Shanice said as she left to call her.

"Bruh, what about Javon?" pried Lucci.

"Zania was trying to say he was mine," Meech frowned as shoveled food in his mouth.

"Stop playing. Get the fuck out of here. That's trifling," Lucci barked.

In between bites, Meech said, "I swabbed little man. It came back he wasn't mine."

"Whew, that one my baby Shanice is carrying, we're definitely testing," Lucci chimed. "I told you, bruh, karma's a bitch. You just got your turn." Meech frowned at Lucci's words which rung truth.

"Damn, bruh still, I gave her a house, car, and plenty paper," a frustrated Meech said.

"Charge it to the game. You're not innocent," Lucci laughed.

From another room, Shanice yelled, "He damn sure isn't."

"Why is your nosey ass way in here?" Lucci joked, folded over in laughter at Meech's dilemma.

"Oh, okay I guess I'm y'all entertainment up here in the boondocks," Meech chimed.

"You fucked up, everyone knows, move on. I hate it for Javon," Shanice responded. "I tried to call her, but only got her voicemail," a disappointed Shanice responded.

"Shit, all that mess I'm sure she's somewhere getting her mind right," Lucci said.

"Well, I see you're in good hands, so I'm outta here. The family just wanted to check on you," Meech said rising up from the table.

"Let me walk you out," Lucci said.

Minutes later, Meech pulled off. "You know your brothers a fucked-up individual, right?" Shanice said sarcastically.

Lucci smiled and said, "Your baby has the same bloodline," as they both walked into the house laughing. "Yeah, he's fucked up," Lucci laughed.

****

Zeneka was sitting in her living room pissed at the latest

revelations and events. Not mad, just surprised that those who should've loved her were her worst enemies. Her tears leaked onto the photo album as she looked at her and Zania's picture wondering how they could be identical twins and be polar opposites. As she was combing through, she also saw pictures of her and Meech, which disgusted her. Zeneka's phone was buzzing. She sighed before speaking.

"Zeneka, hey, it's Rozay. I just wanted to say bye. I'm moving today, and I just wanted to apologize for being an asshole," Rozay apologized.

Sniffling, Zeneka replied, "Fuck you and your apology," as she hung up the phone. She dialed Shanice because she was always her comforter.

Shanice answered, "I called you earlier. How are you?" she questioned.

"I'm surviving, missed you at the proceedings," Zeneka answered sarcastically.

"Your ex-brother-in-law kidnapped me," Shanice joked.

"Did you tell him about the baby," Zeneka countered.

"GGGirl he excited," shrieked a happy Shanice.

"Well, I'm happy for you. Quick question: did you know?" Zeneka questioned.

Silence replaced their rapport. Seconds seemed like minutes. Then Shanice asked, "Did I know what?" Shanice knew she had to distance herself from the Meech and Zania's situation.

"Meech and Zania were sleeping together?"

Shanice had to pour on the theatrics, she let out a gasp.

"OMG," she whined. "Are you serious?" She did it so well that it brought Lucci running.

"What's wrong babe?" a concerned Lucci interjected.

Shanice swatted him away, "Calm down. I'm talking to Zeneka, Mr. Antsy," Shanice teased as Lucci rubbed her stomach and went back to watching his game. "I told you it's like he's a new man," Shanice beamed.

"Those two ain't shit, but that damn Zania," Shanice said sorrowfully.

"Whew, I would've been heartbroken if you knew," a relieved Zeneka said.

"So, how are you and your friend working out?" Shanice pried.

"Fuck all men. I need my space," Zeneka laughed. "When are you coming back? I miss my bestie," she chimed.

"I will be back tomorrow," Shanice confirmed.

"Call me when you get back," Zeneka responded.

"I will as soon as I touch down," Shanice assured her as she ended the call.

****

Earlier that day, Meech served Zania with eviction papers. She had five days to return any property that she received from him. Plus, she was still reeling from the ass whooping Zania had laid on her. Cashmere had really been there for her lately while her world of messiness was caving in. She figured she would invite her out to clear her head. Cashmere would've rather been with Jamari, but he had been busy lately restricting them to phone conversations.

"I thought you were taking your ass home. That was the last thing you said to me before hanging up. What happened to that?" Jamari snapped.

"Babe, chill. My girl going through," Cashmere responded.

"Alright, my bad. Don't let them niggas be in your face," Jamari fumed.

"Boy, bye," Cashmere said. "Umm, I got hungry and drove up to the Golden Crust restaurant that I like so much in the Dilworth area," she calmly told Jamari. They had recently met in the club but hadn't had a chance to hang out.

Cashmere pressed the end button and raced into the restaurant talking as loudly as ever, "I need a red snapper dinner with a fried dumpling and one codfish fritter." Zania looked at Cashmere like she was crazy, then came close enough to smell her. She took one deep whiff of the air and started pointing and acting all crazy.

"You've been smoking. You little liar, you. I thought you gave up that bad habit a long time ago," Zania exclaimed, exposing Cashmere's bad habit.

"Last time I checked, I was grown, and this better not leave this establishment or there'll be hell to pay," Cashmere paused, looking Zania dead in her eyes, "on your part that is. Understand me?" Cashmere sidestepped Zania, leaving her there to ponder if an all-out argument with her friend was the answer right now. She knew everyone's nerves were frazzled from earlier events. Zania concluded the best thing to do was let Cashmere win this argument.

However, she did have to have the last word and mumbled, "Yea, whatever."

Cashmere, having placed her attention elsewhere, snapped back, "Excuse you? I don't think I heard you correctly."

Zania closed her mouth and walked out the restaurant. She was determined not to let this little spat get the best of her. She stood by Cashmere's Chevy when she noticed a blue van parked across the street. Something about this van didn't feel right. It also didn't help that the occupants were staring at her and talking in a tone that was barely audible. She slowly backed up trying to make her way back into the restaurant to advise Cashmere of her thoughts when she bumped into a short, but stocky black male. His physique was that of a gym rat. His mouth uttered, "Oh, I'm sorry miss," while his hands jabbed at her rib cage with a metal object. Zania was ill prepared to defend herself against his brutal attack. As she went to ask him why he had done such a horrible deed to her his simple reply was, "Karma's a bitch."

With those spoken words, he pulled the metal object out of Zania's body and proceeded to walk briskly back to the van as the blood poured from the large, gaping hole he had just cemented in her body.

An unsuspecting Cashmere came outside after the ruckus was over to a battered Zania. She dropped the food packages from her hand and started screaming, "Help! Someone call an ambulance." She tried with all her might to use her body as a brace for her wounded friend. Taking her bare hand, she held it up to the hole in Zania's chest. As the blood poured from Zania's wound and mouth, Cashmere kept asking her over and over again, who could have done this to her. Zania simply responded, "Blue work van." As the words left Zania's lips, Cashmere could hear an engine roar to life. She looked up and caught a glimpse of one of the finest guys she'd ever seen in her life. He gave her a one-dimpled smile then put the van into gear and drove off.

"Was that him, baby girl?" Cashmere asked a weakened Zania.

"Yes," Zania muttered. "He said, 'Karma is a bitch.'"

Zania fainted shortly after alerting Cashmere about the culprit who had harmed her as the ambulance sirens blared in the distance, coming closer. Zeneka convulsed in Cashmere's arms trying to say, 'I love you.'

"Shh, hush baby girl, don't speak. Cash's got you," Cashmere started shaking with rage. She was trying to be strong and reassuring to her best friend as she lie dying in her arms. She realized the ambulance sirens stopped, and she looked up in time to see two EMS workers advancing toward her. Somewhere behind them were two uniformed officers as well.

One of the officers grabbed Cashmere by the elbow and said, "Can you come with me, ma'am?" After getting no response from Cashmere, he spoke to her again, "Ma'am, you have to let them do their job. Come with me. You need to answer a few questions, so we can find out who harmed your friend, ma'am."

Cashmere slowly released Zania into the hands of the capable EMS workers. She followed behind the officer until she heard the female ems worker scream out, "Oh, God, we're losing her!"

Cashmere stopped short and fell to her knees screaming out Zania's name and begging her longtime friend not to leave her.

****

Early the next morning ...

Zeneka was sitting on a park bench when Uncle Absalom sat beside her. "Your situation has been handled," Absalom said as he scattered breadcrumbs for the ducks.

"Huh, what situation?" Zeneka asked as she blew her coffee.

"I heard about the situation with Zania and Meech, and it's being handled. We Barksdales have a code. Meech violated that code. I hate y'all divorced. If you ever need anything just know we are here for you," Absalom said as he scattered the rest of the breadcrumbs in front of the birds and stood to leave. "Take care baby girl."

"You as well, Mr. Barksdale," Zeneka smiled.

Moments later, Zeneka noticed Cashmere calling her phone. She hit the talk button and just listened.

Cashmere frantically yelled, "I been calling you. Zania got stabbed."

Sobbing heavily, Zeneka hit the end button and finished her coffee while watching the birds. "Karma's a bitch," she shook her head. She was basking in Cashmere's announcement and didn't notice Shanice walk up.

"Why are you not answering your phone?" Shanice questioned as Zeneka stood to hug her.

"I'm just enjoying life, no chaser," Zeneka smiled because she was at peace.

"Are you okay?" Shanice pried.

"Yes, bestie, the best I have been in years," Zeneka smiled.

"I'm glad that you are," Shanice smiled. "Hey, Zeneka, don't settle. There are plenty of men who would love to be down for you. There are plenty of men who will be faithful to you. Now trust me there are men that are faithful. Look at Lucci. His whorish ass is trying to change," Shanice giggled.

"Hell no, honey. I would be ghost. I'm too pretty for the B.S.," Zeneka teased.

"I'm tired of seeing you moping over these clowns. I'm tired of seeing you hurt boo," Shanice chimed. "Right now, a man is the last thing on my mind," Zeneka said as she waved away Shanice's comments. "What's crazy is? I still love him." Shanice rolled her eyes and giggled, "Let lying dogs lie." Shanice and Zeneka were busy gossiping when she felt her pocketbook vibrating. She answered. It was

a winded Lucci.

"Baby, where are you?" he said. Shanice's facial expression changed. Zeneka stared, mouthing what's wrong.

"Babe, what's wrong?" Shanice whined.

"I just pulled up to Meech's. Someone burned his house down," Lucci fumed. Zeneka, eavesdropping, smiled to herself.

"Is he okay?" a concerned Shanice asked.

"Yeah, a medic is looking him over now, but his friend, Neeka, wasn't so lucky," Lucci informed her. "I'm sorry to hear that baby," Shanice consoled. "Okay, baby I was just checking on you," Lucci ended. "I'm good. Give Meech my condolences," Shanice emphasized.

"I will. See you at my place later," Lucci chimed as he ended the call.

"Girl, Meech's new house burnt down, and his friend didn't survive," Shanice sympathized as a tear ran down her face. "But you know the damndest thing they also found Rozay dead in the house as well," added Shanice.

Zeneka's face was emotionless as she spoke up, "Karma's a bitch."

****

Luda and Mesha was lounging in Cashmere's secluded apartment waiting for their delivery as they were feeling the effects of the Cali bud they had smoked earlier when the doorbell rung.

"Hey, sis get the door ," yelled Luda who was in the bathroom taking a shit.

Mesha opened the door to a dark-skinned man wearing sunglasses holding a pizza carrier and a Pepsi. "What's the total?," asked Mesha

" It's on the house," he answered as he passed her the soda and the pizza box .

"Well, at least let me give you a tip," flirted Mesha smiling . "No, someone name Vincent took care of it," he assured her.

"Enjoy your meal," he smirked as he turned and walked away. Mesha thought their exchange was odd but just looked at the free food as a hookup.

Luda was now walking out of the bathroom . "What ,I owe you for the food?" he asked Mesha as she sat the food on the table and shook her head, signaling that he owed her nothing. "Well good look out," smiled Luda as he was rubbing his hands together.

"You just finished shitting .I hope you washed your hands," joked Mesha. Luda laughed as he showed Mesha his hands.

"Crack that box open ," responded Luda as Mesha pulled the pizza box towards her. As Mesha opened the lid an explosion blew her head off and killed Luda as well.

Minutes later...

"Hello, this Vincent"

"Yes ,boss this Sweets mission accomplished ,"said Sweets right after he put his muzzle to the real pizza delivery person's head.

"Great job ,you know the routine," said Vincent right before Sweets ended the call.

Nikki Brown PRESENTS

ACCEPTING SUBMISSIONS

You can submit: Urban, Romance, & Contemporary

(Please inquire about other genres)

Submissions@nikkibrownpresents.com

Please email your first 4 -5 chapters as a word doc attachment

Allow 24-48 hours for review

COMING OCTOBER 14TH

Blaire's an attractive woman with two successful businesses, but the one thing she lacks, is love. Her ex Drew, ended their relationship after telling her she was too needy and admitting he cheated. Now that she's single, she decides to just live her life without concerning herself with a man, until she meets handsome James one beautiful summer day, at a gas station.

James is a multi-millionaire, who just so happens to be single, after catching his ex with another man, right on his own couch. James had started to lose faith in finding love again, until he spots Blaire. They instantly click, everything flows easily and James couldn't be happier, but there's just one problem, his old college friend Jessica.

Jessica tried her best to get James to see her as more than a friend, but instead, she ended up watching his love life from the sidelines. Now that James is in yet another relationship, she becomes green with envy and decides she wants him all to herself.

Will a secret from the past interrupt the easy love between Blaire and James or will the love they've built be easily broken?

COMING OCTOBER 22ND

Determination and motivation pays off making Nyla one of the best event planners in the city. She was living her best life until she discovers that her boyfriend Lincoln isn't as stand up as her parents tries to make her believe. Nyla finally frees herself from the unhappiness, deceit and betrayal that lied within their relationship. Knowing that she has to do what's best for her she tries so desperately to move on despite the act of her parents. They try to create doubt and fear in her to keep her from moving.

What she soon felt, but never thought was that the breakup with Lincoln would leave her uninterested with life itself and in her business which was in jeopardy until a new client comes her way giving her the financial stability she so desperately needs to save her business. This is her chance to get back on her feet and prove to herself and her colleagues that she hasn't lost it all.

Sincere has made some life changing decision that caused him to do a long prison stint that left him estranged from his mother who thinks of him now as nothing more than a murder. When he finally joins the free world he quickly discovers that the people in the community and current acquaintances stills hold hatred in their hearts and was looking to get a taste of revenge. The secret of why Sincere went to prison hangs in the balance, and if the truth gets spilled, it won't be the only skeleton coming out of the closet from Sincere's past.

Dom, Sincere's brother is doing what he can to heal the family from the unintentional hurt Sincere caused due to his crime. Dom is truly His brother's keeper. He's a man who is all about doing what he needs to do to get what he wants no matter what the cost is. He always has three main things on his mind at all times family, money and women. One of them will initially change his life for the better.

CPSIA information can be obtained
at www.ICGtesting.com
Printed in the USA
LVHW030219040120
642457LV00011B/879/P